More Happenings
of the
Journeyman

Simple stories from simpler times

*A collection of short stories
set between the 1960s and 1990s,
blending humour, warmth, and life experiences*

Robin E. Bailey

More Happenings
of the
Journeyman

Simple stories from simpler times

First published in Great Britain in 2025
Copyright © Robin E. Bailey
The moral right of the author has been asserted.

Editing, design, typesetting and publishing by UK Book Publishing.
www.ukbookpublishing.com
ISBN: 978-1-918077-43-8

CONTENTS

Also by the author...

INTRODUCTION

The writer is just a simple country boy who entered a unique world of specialist engineering. With that skill developed, he was privileged and trusted to travel the world.

But roots will never be forgotten and with travel similar characters and families ended up not only work colleagues but also close friends.

Sadly, as life moves on so do the various groups of friends, but fond memories give rise to a twist in ideas and hence these stories have been written.

Every aspect of the final story is not just a tale – it is a true happening with only names changed. It is more a brief of the actual events than a story.

Story 1

FALSE ALARM

S usie rolled over and pulled the curtain back. It was still dark outside but looked to be dry. David was still sound asleep, so she eased herself out of the bed and carefully left the room, creeping quietly down the stairs.

She put the kettle on and quickly moved across to the downstairs shower room.

David and Susie had been partners for many years and lived a very dedicated life working together for the Ambulance service. Living on the edge of the very quiet village of Lexton just three miles from the Ravens field town hospital brought them peace and tranquillity after being constantly focused during long working days.

They had obtained the agreement of the supervisor to both work on the same shift, with Susie mainly involved as the operator dealing with all the emergency calls while David was kept on the road. They worked two twelve-hour day shifts and two twelve-hour nights before then having the time off.

Susie finished her shower and made the tea. She took a cup upstairs and carefully woke David, making him aware of the time – as was her usual practice, though not always accurately, then having a quiet giggle because of the panic caused.

She made David a flask of coffee and some beef sandwiches to get him through his day whilst he completed washing the cups with his daily moan about the squirrels.

They are at that bird feeder again, he said. I really don't know why you bother.

Susie never responded – it was David's pet daily moan.

With the village church clock indicating it was half past the hour, they both hurriedly left the house and drove to the depot.

Susie and David had met at university. With both their families heavily involved in the medical profession, neither were allowed to rush through on crash courses. Their parents not only wanted the best for their offspring but wanted them to understand the opportunities that could arise, allowing them to choose a path of study.

Their path through life was virtually decided for them with both knowing what they wanted to do and to feel they would be giving a good service to the community.

They were travelling back to their digs when a motorcyclist drew up alongside. They recognised the rider – a well-liked member of their course, Richard Webb. They could see him grinning through his visor as he started to fool around with first no hands and then getting close to tap on the car window. He then shot off and proceeded to swing the bike from side to side zig-zagging up the road. What he hadn't noticed with his fooling around was the big pothole in the road ahead. His next swing found it and threw him down to the ground and across into the oncoming traffic. A lorry avoided him but the car behind being shielded by the lorry didn't see him until almost on him. The driver on instinct swung towards the verge but caught Richard's leg before crashing into the back of the lorry.

Susie was on her mobile calling 999. They stopped with hazards on and Susie attended to Richard whilst David checked the driver of the car.

Both men were in a bad way but it was due to Susie and David's efforts that bleeding was controlled and bodies made as comfortable as possible before the emergency services arrived that saved them.

At that point both Susie and David knew what their career would be.

Susie made her way to the control. Wished Andy Good Morning whilst he was going through his notes. Helped herself to a coffee as she moved to her desk.

The ambulance hub had room for thirty units but was currently operating with twenty-four. The phones seemed quite quiet at the moment with operators able to at least start conversations amongst themselves.

David was checking his vehicle out and his travelling partner Joe Casson was going through the kit. .

Whilst Joe had finished his paramedic training course, he was nevertheless still in the apprenticeship stage. David was quite fond of Joe, and they were coming together as a very good team. That status is reached when minds are virtually linked with understanding the needs as they treat a victim on site and get them back to the hospital.

It was now 10am and the phones had certainly got busier. Susie picked hers up on the first ring.

Ambulance – what is the problem please.

And what is your name please, sir.

Telephone number?

Address.

Standby, sir, please.

Susie called T3 – Joe answered.

Joe, are you anywhere near Broughton Heath – Co-ordinates through to you now.

About ten minutes, replied Joe.

There is an old barn up Slurry Lane that a team are pulling down. A man has fallen off his ladder and they believe has suffered a broken leg.

I will send through contact details if needed for Charlie Surridge who made the call.

We are on it – said Joe, and the call was done.

Susie reopened the line to Charlie Surridge:

The team will be with you in ten minutes, Mr Surridge, she said. Please make sure access is clear.

Crikey Moses, said David, it's years since I have been near Slurry Lane. We used to sneak up there to meet the girls, played a game called Mummies and Daddies, he added, with a chuckle.

That's why it's called Slurry Lane then, said Joe – avoiding the sharpness of the dig in the ribs.

Well there it is, said David – and that's strange I must say. Why should an old lane like this one in the middle of nowhere and with nothing but a dilapidated old barn at the end of it have a new sign?

Probably taking the barn down to make way for a building site, said Joe. They are building everywhere now. I am going to move to Scotland.

I wish you would was David's reply as they turned in and up the lane.

There was just an old Land Rover parked outside. David swung the ambulance around and reversed up to the barn door.

Two men were waiting with a third standing over another man lying down at a funny angle.

He is over here, said the first man.

David and Joe dropped their bags and knelt beside the man. Joe by his legs and David beside his head. As he bent to ask the normal questions he never got an answer – neither of them did.

After a few moments the barn door was slammed shut and the ambulance drove off. Quickly followed by the Land Rover.

Eleven o'clock on a Monday morning is rarely a busy time for the Lloyds banking facility in Broughton Heath. It was a unique location set back from the road with car parking at the front. Local historians say that it was the headquarters of the army in the First World War. It's certainly prospered since then.

There were just two counters open with four people – two being served and two waiting.

There were two people seemingly writing cheques a short distance apart of a side ledge. One was a policeman who seemed to suddenly be interested in a text.

The two people had now been served and turned to leave as three others came in.

Then the man next to the policeman collapsed to the floor.

The policeman moved quickly over beside him and tried to speak with the man. He rolled him over with arms to the side and checked his pulse. The observers from the counter and the customers were all staring over and the counter clerk turned and undid a side door, allowing her into the main hall.

The policeman was on his mobile.

As the lady arrived he told her an ambulance was on its way and would be here in five minutes. That's lucky, she said, they normally take an hour or more these days.

Please clear the customers and keep the outside free. We need to keep people out and get the ambulance backed up to the door.

The other counter clerk had buzzed for the manager who also now joined them in the hall. The staff ushered the customers out, who, despite some protests were made to understand how serious the situation was. If only they knew. Then they heard the siren and saw the blue light reversing back to the doors.

First the two ambulance men ran through – soon followed by two others – all wearing masks.

The man on the floor suddenly got up and he too put on a mask.

The bank manager and his two duty staff were in shock. The doors to the bank were shut and bolted.

The two men grabbed the manager and forced him back through to his office and out under force to the vaults.

With a number of bags filled, the two men calmly moved back to the front door and waited. The bank's manager and his staff were all tied up and firmly gagged before being carefully moved away.

With a nod across they were ready to reboard the ambulance but needed their member of the police to check outside and keep all clear.

They heard him moving people away and then they carefully unbolted the doors and shifted their bags and comrades into the back of the ambulance. Ambulance doors closed. The bank doors closed, the policeman keeping people back, and the two ambulance imposters got in the cab and with siren and lights ablaze drove off.

Amazingly the policeman had disappeared.

Susie called out across the control room – has anyone heard from T3? she said.

There was a just a shaking of heads.

It's been ages, she said, and so unlike them. I am getting nothing at all. I keep calling and calling.

Radio must have failed, said one – Ok, said Sue, but that does not explain no answer on mobiles. I don't like this at all.

She called across the room again. Does anyone have a vehicle near Slurry Lane? These are the co-ordinates.

No one had any vehicle close and in any event all were involved with instances.

That's it then, said Susie. I am calling the Police. I need them to check this out – something is not right.

PC Jones turned into Slurry Lane and slowly drove up. He noted the tyre marks and judged one was an ambulance. He also noted the barn doors were shut and radioed back to control.

I am outside the barn in Slurry Lane, he said. No ambulance here but tracks indicate that it was here so perhaps still at the hospital. The barn is all closed up.

Ok I will leave now.

The police reported back to Susie who was now more confused than ever and, it must be said, very concerned.

Two lads were wheeling their bikes up the slope from the river at Angle Bridge when they heard what sounded like a radio. They stopped and listened with their fishing rods held tightly across the cross bar.

They carried on up to the road. There was an ambulance parked right near the bridge itself but with all its doors wide open.

T3, T3. Will you please answer – over came another call.

The older lad dropped his bike and rods and ran to the ambulance open door. There was no-one there.

By the way the ambulance had been left he guessed something was wrong.

His mate joined him. It is really odd, he said. Ambulance people are all so particular. Then the radio crackled again. And young Bill climbed aboard.

A lady's voice came through. T3, T3, David this is Susie – Please answer me. Joe, are you there?

Bill fumbled with keys and knobs, saying hello very quietly each time. Then he cracked it. The lady came through again – is that you, T3? The boy repeated what he had done and said: if T3 is an ambulance, yes, this is an ambulance, he replied.

Susie waved to the room and beckoned them over.

What are you doing in an ambulance and what is your name, over.

My name is Bill. This vehicle is empty with doors open. Me and my mate have been fishing and heard the radio.

Where are you? said a desperate Susie. At the Angle Bridge by the river, he said.

Thank you, Bill – now I am going to get the Police to come to you. Please can you stay there.

Yes, said Bill.

Two police cars arrived at the Angle Bridge followed swiftly by Susie.

She explained to the officers who she was and that she was one of the emergency operators at ambulance control and it was her partner and his mate in control of T3.

She was in shock at seeing how the situation was, but keeping calm she thanked young Billy and Tom for their wonderful initiative.

Where are my men? she said in desperation, knowing it was a stupid and futile question.

More officers will be here soon, said Sergeant Boyce, with a consoling hand on her shoulder. We have to be thorough, he said tenderly, so we will be searching the river banks. Also the vehicle will be checked for fingerprints.

Susie could not hold it in any longer. She ran to her car and just broke down in tears.

With a confused crowd waiting outside the Lloyds bank, someone had called the Police. PC Peters pulled over as the groups split up to give him room to park.

There is always someone who takes control of situations and on leaving his car PC Peters was soon informed of events. He walked up to the bank and tested the door. It opened. He called back to the crowd, stating that access was clear and they needed to get in to finalise their affairs with closing time only an hour away. With that he returned this car. As he carefully started to reverse out of the car park, the same man came running out, waving his arms to make him stop.

PC Peters wound his window down whilst containing his patience. Something is wrong in there, the man said. There is no-one there and no-one answers when you try to call for service.

With some reluctance, PC Peters again got out of his car and walked up to the bank. He soon noted how strangely silent and haunting it seemed on the service side.

He called out after pushing the crowd back. He still got no answer. He moved along the counters and noticed a side door. On a slight push it opened. He stepped inside whilst deciding for himself that something was wrong and alerted HQ. Entering places that under normal circumstances he guessed would need keys and combinations, it soon became apparent something serious had occurred. On entry to the vault area, all was revealed.

There had been a serious robbery and the staff had disappeared.

Sergeant Boyce was feeling very concerned about Susie. She was desperately upset and there was little that could be done to comfort her.

A situation he was well familiar with.

With everything organised he moved across to speak with her as she sat in a complete daze in her car. He needed a female police officer to sit with her and was about to arrange that when his mobile rang. He noted before answering it was Superintendent Fuller, so guessed something was serious for him to make such direct contact.

It was indeed serious and threw a completely different light on everything.

With the call ended he spoke with DS Lawrence and informed him of the latest events. Together they walked across to Susie's car. She quickly got out in the frantic hope of some good news.

Miss Smith, said Sergeant Boyce. There has been a development but no news regarding your crew so I need you to accompany me back to the station where we will formally discuss the complete situation. DS Lawrence here will arrange to deliver your car back to the station if you could give him the keys please.

A totally confused Susie started to object, but recognising the change in attitude of both officers she complied.

Susie followed Sergeant Boyce into the station where he directed her to an interview room.

This may seem very formal, said Sergeant Boyce but we have a scenario which is developing – or I should say – has developed into something more serious. In fact very serious. So before we start, can the officer get you a tea or coffee?

Susie just shook her head.

Now, said Sergeant Boyce. I need to get familiar with the whole set of events that you dealt with. All conversations will be recorded but this remains an informal interview at this stage for the benefit of my understanding.

With your involvement recorded I will then advise you on events up to date.

Susie started with the emergency call in.

It was a Charlie Surridge, she said, and continued with reasons for a need and the location.

How was it that it happened to be your partner's team that were directed to the incident?

We hadn't long been in to start our shift, said Sue, so that team was the first obvious choice not to be involved in other emergencies. It turned out they were also closest to the scene.

That was the last contact I had with them. A good while later, having had no contact from the team and they were not responding to my calls which was unusual, I made a call in to yourselves. We had no-one available in the area. Your man reported the site to be clear of vehicles with barn door firmly shut. I was surprised he never entered the building but reported tracks believed to be fresh and belonging to our ambulance.

The next return I got after many frantic calls was thankfully from those lads – we then called you again.

Please, Sergeant Boyce. Tell me everything is ok.

The situation is this, the sergeant replied.

Your ambulance then attended what appears to have been an emergency at the Lloyds Bank in Broughton Heath. Customers were kept clear and the matter was dealt with.

The crowd got impatient and one man rang us to check out why they could not continue with their bank's much needed service .On arrival our man PC Peters just walked up to the bank and opened the door. Everything was clear on the inside so he told the people to just proceed to the counters.

As he was leaving a man ran out quite upset and there appeared to be no service.

Reluctantly PC Peters returned but was faced with the shock of realising the bank had been raided.

Susie just sat there in total shock as the story unfolded further.

There were no bank staff – so what has happened?

The thought then returns to that barn where again two people are missing.

Sadly with suspicious minds the obvious thought is were they all in it together.

No No No, said Susie. And started to protest when the door opened and an officer called Sergeant Boyce out. On his return Susie had her head in her arms lying flat on the table with fists thumping ahead of her.

The sergeant, though a very tough individual, felt so sorry for her. He went round the table. Susie, he said, being very informal. We have had forensics on the phone and with their methods checking out all facilities the bank staff have been found, the two women bound and gagged in the ladies' toilet and the manager in the gents'. They are in shock of course and quite weak but are giving statements now. You and I need to check out that barn in Slurry Lane. As a precaution, can you set up an ambulance crew to be there – just in case.

With a positive purpose once again, Susie was in action and all from her side was organised and she sat with Sergeant Boyce on a fast ride to Slurry Lane. Forensics had been called and alerted they may be needed there.

Susie found it strange – she was buzzing once again as her life's duties kicked in again but with a personal focus in hand.

A squad car was already at the barn and had swung the bar across and then dragged the door open but disappointment awaited. The place appeared to be empty.

Sergeant Boyce and Susie stood in the centre just looking around them with Susie becoming quite distraught.

Without thinking and in totally uncontrolled desperation, she screamed out – David, where are you, before falling to the floor. But Sergeant Boyce had heard something and ran to the back of the barn where a thick layer of straw bales lay.

Over here, he yelled to the other officer as the ambulance arrived. Bleary eyed, Susie got up and quickly joined Sergeant Boyce. He was kicking back dirty old bails, revealing both ambulance men firmly tied and gagged.

Susie couldn't contain herself and in floods of tears hugged the tied up bundle that was her David. But she was pulled back by Sergeant Boyce and the Ambulance crew. These men need to be released and laid out quickly, he said The paramedics' decision finding their mates had low blood pressure, temperature and faint heartbeats was to get them back to the hospital without further delay.

The police interviewed the bank manager who advised them how professional the ambulance men had been. They had given no indication that they were imposters. He was very concerned as to how they seemed to know the exact layout of his bank plus its monetary status.

This bank only had large funds delivered in at odd times. It seemed to him like an inside job, but he said that could only be supposition.

The forensic team finished their work with the thanks and praise given by the two ladies for finding them.

The bank remained closed.

David had recovered from his ordeal well, but Joe remained in intensive care.

As the story unfolded giving David the full picture of events, it became clear both men had been attacked with a fast-acting chloroform rag but Joe it seemed had been well overdosed. Any later and an assault and robbery would have been upgraded to murder and robbery. As it happens, Joe may still not regain his full faculties.

There were no clues. David soon regained his strength and was subject to a lot of Susie's attention – now known as matron.

Three days passed and Joe was in the recovery ward.

David sat by his bed and gave him the full story from their arrival at the barn. Their treatment and the events that followed.

There are no clues – no evidence – no nothing for the police to go on. It's just mystifying.

It was so well planned. They even tied and gagged all of us and made sure we were well hidden to gain full getaway time.

They say it must have been an inside job.

Joe moved forward and with a weak hand pulled David close to him.

I believe it's all my fault, he said. I remember clearly now, he said. Before the world went blank I recognised one of the men. Although all masked he had a unique scar just under his eye. When I say unique it is straight with odd criss crosses and almost like a tattoo. He was a good friend from schooldays. Him and his girlfriend wanted to learn how to become one of us. I was proud to show him especially as he was so keen – the questions rolled in almost daily. He seemed particularly interested in the operation of the Ambulance itself.

What is his name? David asked.

Timothy Walsh, Joe replied. He lives in that remote old bungalow not far from Angle Bridge. He has a truly gorgeous girlfriend – Anthea Morris. She works in Lloyds up in the city.

David shot out of the room and rang Susie.

Susie, you have Sergeant Boyce's number, don't you. Tell him to meet me at the hospital and give him my number. I think Joe has given us some vital information.

Sergeant Boyce certainly was over the moon with getting a link at last and gave his sincere thanks to Joe for living long enough to remember the information – giving Susie a sly wink.

The past few days had been quite a strain for all.

Six months later Timothy and Anthea were returned to the UK – nicely bronzed but that was soon to fade. The rest of their team had been picked up earlier.

The exact size of money involved was never disclosed but it certainly was a substantial sum. The five-man team were subjected to a fifteen-year jail term whilst the woman got off with a warning because of insufficient proof but lost her job with Lloyds.

Susie was happily doing her operational bit. David and Joe having their usual rounds of banter whilst travelling to the next emergency.

Then their radio went.

Hi Joe, said Susie.

I have some co-ordinates needing a quick visit – can I send them to you?

Go ahead, said Joe.

Got them, he said and no – we are certainly not going there.

He could hear the laughter coming from the control room not helped by David giggling away.

T3 no like Slurry Way, he said.

Story 2

COURSING

T he village of Kirston was normally a very quiet sanctuary but today was slightly different with four Land Rovers towing heavily laden trailers travelling through and chugging their way up to Wintry Lane.

John Masters was expecting them and had clearly signed the turning into Slade Farm.

The sun was shining. It was a lovely spring day with the birds happily getting their nests ready – the squirrels being more nosey than ever and the rabbits in and out of the hedge line.

John was out in the yard and gave the thumbs up as the first trailer slowly passed by him to make room for the rest as they left the lane.

The farm was set back in the quiet East Anglian countryside. A beautiful location on the edge of a small valley shielded by the trees of Lucy Wood.

John had inherited it from his parents and was now planning the many improvements as considered necessary by the young when taking over from the old.

There was, however, an urgency with completing those improvements, with marriage planned for the end of the year when his partner finished her term of study at the Wageningen University and research in Holland.

A happy clash would then once again be developed between a skilled and heavily qualified horticulturalist and one of a plain agricultural background. The competition would be quite fierce with extensive greenhouses planned by the one and expanded acreage planned by the other.

The four Land Rovers were to be the start for speeding up the natural farming process. Their purpose being to link the flat lands up with the valley.

Most of the farm crop yielding land was inaccessible directly from the farm due to the presence of a fast-flowing stream running along the base of the small valley. That stream involved hours of lost time driving to its nearest crossing point.

With speed being of the essence, the clever notion of a bridge had been planned.

With planning approved and agreed the team had arrived.

Mark Leigh jumped down from his Land Rover and stretched his legs before marching quickly over to John Masters. It's good to see you again, Mark, said John, as they firmly shook hands.

We are The Bridge and Special Crossings company – at your disposal, said Mark with a mock salute.

Let me introduce you to the crew. With no bosses unless the chips are down – this is Jimmy – the lone Ranger; Freddie – Jimmy's guardian. Then there is Dan,

Charlie and Phil. As you know a longstanding firm team. Let's go to the point of duty.

John – can you confirm that this is the place you want it?

Indeed, it is, said John.

So we will stick to the council limit and measure off 4.5m as the maximum width, said Mark. We are ok on the maximum 9m length – or rather width of crossing.

We have a pontoon on board. A 5-tonne tracked digger with a 4" pump – just in case needed – is due anytime.

You said before that we can use your facilities so no need for a welfare truck.

Yes, said John. Just let me know if extra's needed.

Right, leave it with us and we will set to with marking it all out to get started, said Mark.

Can Charlie and Phil come with you to see where the facilities are please, John?

Of course, said John, and turning with a wave of the arm said, follow me back to the house.

The excavation on the South side had gone well. John stopped by to check if anything was needed before moving on to check the North side.

That's some vehicle you've got there, said Mark. You never had that when I came before.

It's a weakness of mine, said John. I just love the Range Rovers – their strength with comfort – their reliability.

Mark grinned his agreement – Enjoy, he replied.

With everything marked out, digger in place and pump at the ready, things were moving ahead quite nicely.

God it's taking John some time to get to North side, said Mark.

He has probably driven off smitten by his new Range Rover and forgetting the rest of the world exists, said Freddie.

But then a very unhappy John returned. His vehicle was a mess.

What the hell's happened to you, said Mark as the whole crew stopped work and moved quickly over to the Range Rover. Its sides were battered. Windscreen cracked. Front and rear damage quite evident.

John was in bits – almost in tears as he got out.

It's those bloody hare coursers, he said. Travellers arrive every year and just run riot across our land. They have no regard for anything or anybody.

But hare coursing is illegal, said Mark.

John ignored Mark's statement.

Today it's six travellers, another day it could be 56 travellers. Violence is second nature. They run riot and nobody cares. Dog walkers run away from them.

It is illegal but the police never come.

I just asked them to leave and this was the answer I got.

Then you must report it to the police, said Jimmy.

I inferred the fact they were on private land and breaking the law so the police could be called. Their reply was to make sure a fire engine and an ambulance also attended as my farm would be burnt down. With the thumping they then gave my vehicle I got the message and got myself away.

I will just have to live with it each year and ignore them with no other support.

I think I will go up to the house now and have a large whisky.

Mark and the team had grown to like John. They had worked together for quite some time getting designs ready and meeting the council inspectorate on site alongside the river authorities. In the end the width and length rule was applied and now a week's work would see it just needing to settle before use.

Are you ok carrying on, Jimmy, if I go up and see if John's ok, said Mark. It's obviously hit him and he has taken it very hard.

Go, said Jimmy. But don't say too much. I know you too well and feel tension once again in the air.

Are you there, John, said Mark as he stood by the kitchen door.

I'm just in the lounge came the reply – just come straight in.

Mark took his boots off and tiptoed across to the lounge.

Seeing John, sitting there seemingly gazing into space, left Mark – as hard as he was – engulfed with sympathy.

Look, John, he said. What has happened today could have happened to anybody and the reason such happenings occur is because nothing is done about it. So the bullies return year after year and in greater numbers and for longer times.

What has happened to you today will never happen again – I can assure you of that. So pull yourself together now. We have a bridge to complete – and I then have a further challenge. You have to be ready for a female's return and in preparation I suggest you make an advance booking with a marriage counsellor.

That did bring a smile to John's face.

So the aim now, said Mark – is to rise above it.

I am going back to the bridge now – but leave the rest with me.

John just nodded but had not picked up on the message Mark had given him.

The bridge they were fitting was a second-hand MOD heavy duty number 12 military pair of units. They were a link up design for the advance of heavy military vehicles. The team were well familiar with those and they would be firmly fitted in place well before the end of the week. The two sections were 13.5m long and 1.5m wide. Perfect for farm use with all plant.

With the concrete bases now installed in readiness on both sides of the stream the team cleared the area in readiness for the final placement tomorrow. Leaving the time necessary for the concrete to set properly, the plant was put off hire and the team left site.

The travellers returned to their camp in 'Monks Field', getting two hares ready for skinning whilst putting the dogs away. Their arrogance left them totally unaware that they were being watched. Under surveillance would be the true terminology for the coming events.

The team were at Slade Farm early the next day. The two sections were winched into place and fixed. Job complete and ready for the test. John was ecstatic. His tractor was close by and a bottle ready to smash at the start to declare the bridge as open. It was perfect and with a new route formed, the agricultural traffic would be fairly constant.

That's brilliant, said John. Just let me know what I owe you and your bill will be paid.

So what's the programme with those coursers, said Jimmy as Mark turned away, trying not to make the question having too obvious a need for accurate answers.

If they follow their normal programme they will move onto Lord Lydon's fields – probably next week. They seem to follow a pattern across the county and with the timing normally the same you really would think the police would be ready and adopt some form of control.

Surely Lord Lydon would take action.

For God's sake, said John. He is a Lord. He is rarely here and his staff are not interested. They enjoy a quiet life keeping the estate running in low profile. The last thing they want is threats or smashed vehicles to upset their cosy lives.

Not bitter by any chance then? said Mark with a chuckle – a point ignored by John.

What route do they take then? said Jimmy.

Straight off the point where my land links at the Kirston/Conway crossroads and straight across the fields from there directly to the church.

A Holy end to their season no doubt before they return to Ireland, grunted Mark.

On that note the team all said their goodbyes. Mark made the point that both he and Jimmy would drop by at some stage later on to check all was ok, and with that they left.

Surveillance continued at the travellers' site but now things were changing as the dogs were becoming the focus of more attention. Something was in the planning and the time had come.

The next morning the travellers' site was a buzz of activity. So unusual for such an energy display. The weather was good with sun shining and no wind. With dogs loaded, four vehicles left and continued down to the Kirston crossroads. John was right – the next round of coursing was now underway across the hallowed territory of Lord Lydon.

The dogs were released and the first truck took off. A minute or so later the second, then the third and finally the fourth. So with a line of vehicles with respective hunter dogs the hares must take flight. But not today.

It seemed that all the trucks had reached various stages of swerve and stop. For any onlooker that would seem very strange, but the answer soon revealed itself with the fourth truck as the example.

The traveller got out and walked around to the front offside tyre. It was flat. As he bent to check it further a foreign voice command rang out. You vill sit on the floor now – it demanded.

In anger the traveller turned to be faced with a figure in a grass cloak, blackened masked face and carrying a pretty heavy rifle.

The traveller lurched forward but was thrown to his left and the gun fired a quiet round, clipping the side of his knee.

Move back – the figure said and take off your clothes.

Now the traveller was in shock – but never moved.

Sacre Bleu came the response as another round was fired to clip past the other knee. If no clothes off then next shot will be actual knee – your choice.

The traveller with wary eyes slowly disrobed but stood in shock as an explosion could be heard followed by a fire up the field.

Put your clothes in your vehicle, the figure demanded, and step away.

With a trickle of blood running down both legs and bare feet suffering, the traveller was no longer the fearsome animal he claimed to be. More fear followed as his vehicle was hit by an object thrown by the figure and instantly burst into flames.

Now you have learnt your lesson, the figure said; ve are the protectors of this land and its vildlife. Ve look after this county. Ve have teams in other counties.

Enter lands that belong to nature and kill the natural habitat, and you will die next. Now get moving. The open field is yours so freedom you have – just like an animal. You have a five-minute window before I hunt you down…GO.

The traveller started to run with great difficulty toward the other three vehicles which were all in flames.

The figure moved quietly back and disappeared.

The travellers' camp was quiet – seemingly deserted but with three ladies approaching, the doors from each van soon opened.

With an aggressive stance the first lady challenged the arrivals.

They were foreign with strange markings on their faces.

Ve are the cleaners and the carers of these lands. Ve need to purify your homes to make them safe for the future.

The occupants were all totally confused as the ladies produced rods with bottles near the base and each proceeded to spray along the roof of their nearest van. With anger in the camp as they moved around each van, reactions soon occurred and moves swiftly made to get them off site.

John was halfway across the stream and feeling on top of his world when he noticed smoke in the distance. Not that it would normally warrant more than a glance but streaming up from four equally spaced locations it did seem odd for this time of the year.

As he pulled into the yard Jasper Lucas – Lord Lydon's gamekeeper – arrived, giving the appearance of some distress.

Sorry to bother you, John, he said, but have you sent any vehicles across our land for any reason?

Of course not, said John. What kind of question is that. Don't you think if I had spare vehicles I would go by road or ask you first?

Yes, stuttered a completely confused Jasper – a person taken completely out of his daily mundane routines by an event outside the ordinary. But there are four vehicles across our fields and all are in flames. Aside from that, we have nudists running around.

John suppressed a chuckle. Are you sure you haven't been drinking or eaten the wrong mushrooms, Jasper, he said.

It's true, John. What should I do?

Contact his Lordship – let him test your sanity, John replied. But then he remembered seeing the four lines of smoke.

Ok, Jasper – apologies – I did see some smoke so I think you should phone the Police.

Jasper nodded and quickly left.

John shook his head with an uncontrolled lonely giggle seeing the pathetic figure of Jasper driving off.

It was PC Adams who took the call at the Conway Police headquarters. He turned to his Sergeant – it seems there is a problem up at Lord Lydon's estate at Kirston, and he explained the content of Jasper's uncanny call.

Can we be sure it's not a scam call was the initial response, but then another call came in about seeing vehicle fires in the estate fields.

I think we will both go, said Sergeant Croft.

John was still chuckling to himself when Mark and Jimmy arrived.

Ok, so what's the joke? said Mark – Bridge collapsed and madness set in? – or something similar!

Something similar is right, said John.

I have just had that loon around from Lord Lydon's estate reporting nudists running around with fires burning in the fields.

Oh a modern take of the paganist age. Well that is something different which could catch on, said Jimmy.

So how is the bridge?

It's perfect, said John. Can't wait to take the combine over it. A real tester.

More a test of your driving than the bridge itself, said Mark, suffering a scowl from John.

If nothing is needed we will leave you in peace then, they said and left.

As they drove off to the Kirston crossroads they gently pulled over to let the police car get by with a brisk wave of acknowledgement from Sergeant Croft.

As the police car travelled up the drive to the manor they could detect the stench of a weird smoke-laden atmosphere. They turned in front of the main entrance where Jasper Lucas was clearly parked and waiting for them.

Are you ok following me out into the fields? he asked. It is dry and firm out there so you shouldn't have a problem.

Lead the way, said Sergeant Croft. I think it best we get more support out here. Was it you who reported nudists floating about?

Yes, said Jasper. I have seen three so far – all male I might add.

Oh that's a disappointment then, said an impatient looking Sergeant Croft – rolling his eyes and creating a smirk from PC Adams.

Having radioed in and got the ok from Superintendent Bowles, more squad cars were on their way.

As they approached the first vehicle, both the sergeant and his PC were quietly aware this was not going to be a simple case. Something was amiss and seeing other burnt-out wrecks in the distance made Sergeant Croft report in again.

I think we have a serious incident here, Sir, he said. We are going to have to seal off the area and get forensics involved. Burnt out vehicles could be concealing bodies – we have yet to check.

As he finished the call he was aware of a lady in some distress running up the field towards them.

That's Martha the housekeeper, said Jasper jumping in his vehicle to drive down to her.

As he turned beside her she was very distraught. There's a nude man in the house, she said. He just ran in – pushed me over the table and ran up the stairs. We need the police down there now. She was gasping for breath and panting fiercely as Jasper helped her into the truck. He drove back to the wreck and informed the Police before turning back to the Manor. The police quickly followed with alerts sent out.

A second squad car had just arrived with surprise at the strange activity as Jasper with PC Adams ran into the house.

Sergeant Croft informed him of events as Jasper returned to say the bedroom wardrobes had been ransacked but Lady Lydon's estate car had been stolen.

An estate passed me on the drive up, said PC Webster. I thought it was a bit erratic.

Have you the registration, Sir, please, said Sergeant Croft as he turned to Jasper.

With that given an alert was put out.

The traveller was well dressed in Lord Lydon's finery as he raced back to camp. His aim was to collect his wife and run for it. The others would either have gone or would follow. They had lost nearly everything so the need to escape was a desperate one.

Then a second shock hit him. All the women were standing outside their vans and in tears. He jumped from the vehicle and ran to his wife's side. She was hysterical and so angry with him – Why have you all destroyed us, she screamed. The others echoed her screams and then he saw the reason. Each van had suffered terrible damage. Something seemed to have eaten away the metalwork and every van's roof had fallen in.

Whilst the shock hit him there was nothing more he could say as two police cars arrived and blocked the site.

It seemed that John was always crossing his bridge when visitors arrived. It was almost timed as a show of – come and see my new crossing but this time it was a police car.

Hello Sir – Are you the resident here? I am PC Matthews.

Hi, said John – Yes – How can I help?

We are investigating some vehicle fires on Lord Lydon's estate but also reports of nudists running around the area. Have you seen or heard anything?

John confused the Police constable as he laughed in recollection of the earlier visit from Jasper. PC Matthews fully understood when John explained the situation from the earlier Jasper visit and a brief resume of the character.

So you haven't seen any nudists, said the PC suppressing a grin. What about vehicles?

Nothing has passed through here, said John. I only have that Range Rover and the only other vehicles that have been here today were the bridge erectors.

That Range Rover has taken a bashing. What happened there – it's virtually new.

Oh it was over a week ago we had the normal annual Hare coursers running through. I challenged them and that's what I got.

Why didn't you call us, said PC Matthews – Hare coursing is illegal.

I know it is, said John, and when I said that I could be calling you they advised me to call a fire engine and ambulance at the same time as they would be burning my farm down. Just for good measure they then attacked my new vehicle – hence No – I daren't call you.

That explains a lot – I now need to get back to my Sergeant.

With that PC Matthews left.

A few days later the matter of the happenings on the Lord Lydon estate was being discussed in superintendent Jones office.

It had gradually become clear that the vehicles were not stolen. They belonged to the travellers.

Checks were being made on the number plates for legality and any other possible issues, but the main point was focussed on their reasons for being in the fields and what happened in those fields.

It was obvious hare coursing was the activity, particularly since two lurchers and two greyhounds were collected by the kennel people from outside the Kirston Pig and Whistle pub.

Their abode was rough old kennels at the travellers' Monks Green site.

So, said the Superintendent. In a nutshell, they were breaking the law. Upsetting many landowners each year throughout the country. Whilst it is illegal we never have the staff to deal with it so it is always left to run its course. Somewhere along the way landowners have taken action. No one has been hurt. In reality, the law has been restored and may now remain that way with the travellers given a strong dose of their own medicine.

So I suggest we allow the vehicles now to be cleared off Lord Lydon's fields, scrapped and we declare the matter closed. I don't think those travellers will be placing any claims.

I assume we can support Slade Farm when they claim insurance on that Range Rover – and I must have a word with their Bridge Builder. They were special forces you know.

Story 3

ANTIQUES TURNED

A s age creeps up on us all, our list of possessions also grows over those years.

My father was a bricklayer. His parents owned a pub with a small farm attached. They were totally self-sufficient with all the family well taken care of with – in reality – little need to attend the village school. Their education was in the land.

Grandfather had two carthorses. He was an amazing man as every Wednesday he would select one horse with cart then trot into town to the cattle market. It was no short distance – some eleven miles.

Then by late afternoon his friends would lift him back on his cart – drunk as a skunk – and with a smack on the rear the old carthorse would trot slowly back to the farm. The equivalent of a homing pigeon in the animal world.

I had passed the eleven plus which segregated me from all my mates with attendance at the all-boys grammar school as opposed to the boys enjoying the girls in the secondary modern.

Dad hated doing it, but every Friday night he took on serving at the pub as a relief for his brothers and sisters, plus it made my gran happy. But by golly he must have been the most grumpiest barman in the country.

Sadly, as I was sitting my A levels my grandfather died. He was a good age and really considering he never suffered at the age of ninety-five he was very lucky. The funeral was well attended at the local church and Gran wore black from that day onwards.

She used to sit beside the old black fire with the huge food table so close by that everyone had to walk around to get to her. That was the way they were and the way it would continue.

I was getting prepared to go to the youth club that evening when Aunt Doris turned up on her bike. Mother called me from downstairs, and unknown to me at the time, my first real challenge in life was about to begin.

Hi Aunt Dorry, I said – Nice to see you.

Nice to see you too, David, she replied. You are like the invisible man these days. Got a girlfriend, have we?

He better not have, my mum quickly said – determined to get her five penneth of control in. Your Aunt Dorry is here with a request from your gran, she continued.

The mystery was beginning to get to me with the youth club beckoning.

Well, all of us back at the farm really, said Dorry. Not just your gran.

We have been clearing out a lot of your grandad's things and at the same time collected together a lot of – well quite frankly – junk. But your gran thinks there could be some value there and has asked the antique dealer to call by. It's all old pottery, some ancient old cookery stuff, tools and things. She calls you the brainy one of the family and wants to see if you would come along and attend to the dealer.

Of course, I said, but when?

Saturday at ten o'clock, Aunt Dorry replied.

Well it's lucky it's half term, I said, because I really need to get familiar with everything. I will pop up tomorrow if that's ok.

Perfect, said Aunt Dorry.

Ok, I will be up there about ten, I said. Must go now – youth club calls.

With the normal goodbyes I left.

I arrived at the Green Star pub just after ten. Gran welcomed me with arms outstretched for the normal hug in her chair. After the usual chat and with the latest village gossip relayed, I asked her who was coming and where would I find the sales items.

They are all in the barn, Gran said. It's Charles Oates from the Oates Antique shop in town, with his son Graham.

I scowled at the thought of seeing his son again. A mister Hoyty toyty in private education and a spoilt brat.

You just don't like his son, do you, David? said Gran.

He is just so spoilt and arrogant, I replied.

I believe it's a number of years since you have seen him, said Gran. You could be pleasantly surprised. Nonetheless, put any personalities to the back of the mind. We need you to get a fair deal.

I left Gran and went to the barn. There was quite a bit of stuff there and really should not be just left in an open barn.

There were small figurines which I knew were his collection of fairings. I must get a book from the library on those, I thought.

Several old teapots. A very large kettle – black as the ace of spades. Old bottles Grandad had obviously dug up over the years.

Some lovely pictures – mainly landscapes – and then quite a number of garden tools. All very aged and ideal for a medieval movie.

I returned to the house.

Now, Gran, I said, you cannot leave all that stuff out there in an open barn. The tools yes – but the rest – no. We need to get it in here. Agree between ourselves and have a plan. Whatever happens they are dealers and will try and rip us off. I suggest you put them off for a week and let them stew. They will be well aware there are goods worth having and some to give them a good profit.

Glad I called you, David, she said. I will do as you say. I will get Harry to bring them all up and set them up in the lobby. He will be told to lay all the tools out in the barn.

Let me know when they are all in place, I said, and I will come up and take some pictures. I do need time to check some things out.

Now I warn you. If there is something really valuable in their eyes they will get quite pushy and their manner will change. If we recognize that then we tell them we have a second dealer coming in and will let them know our decision in due course.

Their reaction to that should be interesting.

I returned the next day having got the message that Harry had set everything up in the lobby. The polaroid was ready. With a change made to the layout, I left and cycled into town to the library. There were several books on Fairings and all that Grandfather had were indeed listed. Values were indicated in one book which was a godsend. There were many antique books but few values shown. It was difficult to make any true assessment of other values.

I decided to contact my close mate Kevin. His father worked in London and was well connected. Despite the crackly line I managed to get the message across to him and would get some polaroids over to him for his father to hopefully be able to get checked out.

And so the Saturday arrived and tension within the Green Star mounted.

As I watched them park up and walk up towards the main entrance, I couldn't help grinning to myself.

I thought you said that son Graham had grown up, Gran, I said.

Don't start, David, she said. Concentrate on the job in hand. We are relying on you.

Sorry, I mumbled.

There was a brisk Tap tap…tap on the door which I duly opened.

Good morning, said the taller of the two.

We are Charles and Graham Oates from Oates Antiques. We are here to see Mrs Jacobs if you wouldn't mind taking us to her.

I am David Jacobs, I replied. I shall be handling matters on behalf of my grandmother, but I will introduce you to her if you follow me.

I will show you the pottery and other stuff first, which is in the other room, and then we will go out to the barn.

We will follow you then, said Charles glancing across to his son.

There are a number of teapots, I said, and then this collection of Fairings.

He loved his Fairings did my Grandad and these are becoming quite popular.

Don't know about that, said Charles, but we shall see.

They went through the cluster on the table and Charles looked across to young Graham.

Doesn't seem to be much of value here, he said, ignoring the guide.

I suppose the old teapot could be worth a pound or two, replied the young Graham – again ignoring the host.

Well take us to the barn, said Charles.

I turned and led the way out.

The barn was different. The observations made of their smug ways was quietly amusing but in reality quite sad. They had picked up the big old pitch-black kettle. It had obviously been used in many open fires to get as black as that. The son was picking into the black near to the base.

Thinking I would not notice the glance between him and his father which was quite obvious in what it meant. Then they turned and suddenly attitudes changed with great excitement with arms pointing and both moving towards a broken arm off one of Grandad's old trailers.

This is in the sale, isn't it, said Charles.

If it interests you then for sure, I said knowing full well it was an act.

Right. I think we are finished here and need to go back and talk with your Gran, said Charles.

I looked him straight in the face and replied coldly and firmly. It is me you are dealing with; and noted the Graham arrogant expression as he turned away.

Ok, said Charles. The only thing of any value to us here is that shaft over there. The rest is just odds and sods.

For the shaft we will give twenty-five pounds and two pounds for that old kettle – mainly because its size may be of interest to someone in their garden. The rest …well we will bring the total up to thirty pounds.

Then if we say twenty for the crockery in the house that will round it up to fifty pounds.

Really, I said. Well we better get back to the house and you can re-think on that pottery.

I was seething inside so when we got to the door and they started to walk through I called them sharply back and pointed to the mat. Take your shoes off please. They are covered in mud.

Sheepishly they returned, bringing me much pleasure as I slipped through for a quick quiet word with Gran.

Then I waited by the open door to again lead them across to the room with the pottery bits and pieces.

They pretended to show no interest in the fairings and again concentrated on the teapot, stating with some reluctance they could offer another pound. With that I turned and took them back to collect their shoes. The appearance of them tiptoeing through whilst holding their dirty shoes seemed to have reduced their arrogance.

In the lounge I called across to Gran. They have finished the viewing, I said.

Then of course Lord Charles had to go forward and present his arrogant spiel with an offer that could not be matched, to Gran.

Oh that is very kind of you, Mr Oates, she said. We will give that some thought.

But we are ready to take it all away with us now – after all, it is a long way from town and we can't really afford more days away from the shop.

Well don't worry, said Gran. We will let you know in a week or two when the other lot have done their valuations.

But – I thought, he spluttered.

I interrupted him saying that I would see them both out.

As they put their shoes back on outside the front door, Charles turned to me. Another tenner should see the deal closed if you agree, he said.

Sorry, I replied, it's my gran's decision, isn't it, and with that I firmly shut the door.

You did well there, Gran, I said.

You think I would make a good actress then? she said. So come on, I did as you said, so why and what was the outcome?

I told her everything. Helping her to understand that they really are cheats and confidence tricksters. With particular reference to the attempted con with the old cart shaft in the barn and the possible real value of the kettle.

There is something about that kettle, I said, so I am going to check that out. They scratched it near the base and suddenly could not conceal some renewed interest.

You know why? said Gran – it's copper.

Well that says it all, I said. With that and the fairings – they are just a pair of conmen.

I am going to take some more photos and get my best mate Malcombe, Kevin's twin brother, to give them to his dad to check out for us. He works in the city and has a good set of contacts.

Meanwhile, I will do some checking into things myself.

I went home and with some excitement picked up my camera. Life was suddenly very interesting, and I was on a mission.

With photos taken and copies given to Malcombe, I recovered the old kettle from the barn and started to check out copper kettle values. That was when the shock in the form of a very pleasant surprise hit me. That kettle when properly cleaned up to its original status could be worth anything up to six hundred and fifty pounds.

Next it's the fairings, but first a visit to friends in the steel fabrication business. So another school mate was brought into the equation. I need a dummy double.

Malcombe's dad did me proud. He confirmed that one teapot was quite valuable – the fairings varied from just a few pounds to four hundred pounds but two were copies and worth virtually nothing. He confirmed my findings on the kettle.

The steel fabricators did a superb job with a brilliant copy and made heavy duty. A tenner and a bottle sealed that favour.

Paul the local blacksmith soon sorted the last phase with a completely black lookalike with a twist of copper stuck in place and an outside scratch to complete its reveal.

I briefed Gran – it was time to invite the Oates lot back – if indeed still interested; but they were firmly told over the phone that one teapot had been smashed and the fairings would not be included. The rest they could have for seventy five pounds.

The deal was done. Two very happy dealers left with their conning shaft worth nothing and that valuable kettle plus the rest of the bits and pieces excluding those fairings.

The fairings and the kettle were later sold at an auction house via Malcombe's dad, in the city for the princely sum of sixteen hundred pounds after commission paid.

Malcombe and his dad were given a cool hundred plus the travel expenses.

Then Malcombe's dad could not resist visiting Oates Antiques where he saw a black kettle.

It's a genuine copper kettle worth six hundred pound, but five ninety to you, Oates said.

With a scratch near the top, Malcombe's dad had great satisfaction proving it to really be a valueless old rusty steel kettle.

It would have been good to have filmed the Oates family reactions of horror, embarrassment and dismay.

But this time the conners had been conned.

Story 4

THE DEAR MISS ELLIS

M iss Ellis was a happy lady. An aging spinster but young at heart. A friend to all and always there when help was needed.

Young Freddie Nelson needed help now as he received another slight rap across the knuckles for hitting yet another wrong note today.

As nice as Miss Ellis was, she lived for her pianoforte and had taught many youngsters – always with the serious intention of getting them through their Grades – right up to Grade 8.

Now, Freddie, stop. What is wrong with you today – anything worrying you that I should know about? she asked.

No, Miss, said Freddie as the door opened and his mother walked in.

Miss Ellis turned and smiled at Cherrie. He is not performing today, she said. I have asked him to just warm up and run through the scales as normal, but his left hand seems to trail behind his right. Sadly, it would be safe to say not many wrong notes have been missed either throughout this session. He has just not been himself today. Anyway – we all have our off days – how has your week been, Cherrie, she asked?

Same as normal really, Cherrie replied. Gerald has been working away so freedom and peace reigned, but he is back now so it's football, football and more flipping football. I tried to attract his attention, since he had been away all week, and asked him if he had ever felt like giving anyone a hug or perhaps a little cuddle. You would not believe his reply.

Freddie was starting to giggle.

Go on, said Miss Ellis. I assume he cracked your ribs with the force of it ruining the thought of any further actions.

Cherrie pointed to Freddie – even he was in shock, she said.

His reply was a yes – when Mark Jones scored the winning goal at Greenwich. I just could not believe it.

With the small room now recovered and in tune with laughter, Cherrie pushed a giggling Freddie out of the door, and they left to get the bus home.

Miss Ellis was still chuckling to herself as she too got her bags ready and left to catch the bus into town. Today was shopping day.

The bus pulled up outside Number 25 Broad Street and a grateful Miss Ellis thanked the driver and said her goodbyes. Several people waved as she walked across to her gate and the bus drove off.

The driver turned to the lady in the front seat. She is a lovely lady her, he said. I always drop her off at her home when I'm on.

I agree with you, the lady said. And she does so much to help people. She is a music teacher, you know. She has got my Jimmy up to his third grade. She is so patient.

Miss Ellis put her bags down and tilted the plant pot back to get her door key. It wasn't there. Troubled and confused, she looked up and then with some relief saw it was in the door. With no further concern she considered it to be her forgetfulness and reminded herself to double check next time she left her house. The thought never entered her head that something was wrong or that a burglar may still be inside. She was simply old school – trusting and naively innocent.

She went inside and put her shopping away, made herself a cup of tea and sat wearily down on the sofa. Everything was in order. It had been a good day. Tomorrow is Saturday with three lessons to get through so an early night was called for.

It was 9.30 on the Saturday morning that the first victim arrived. It was Mark Timms – known by all as Tubby Timms for obvious reasons. Always nibbling something.

Welcome, John, said Miss Ellis. So you are the escort for young Mark here today. Your good lady not well?

She is fine, said John. Made me come with her today. She is enjoying the freedom of the town and emptying the shops.

Miss Ellis gave a knowing nod as she took young Mark's coat and sat him on the stool in readiness for his thirty-minute session.

John quietly left, saying he would be back in an hour.

Miss Ellis loved Saturdays. She always had a house full as the young population grew waiting for parents to return.

John had just turned out of the gate when he heard an urgent call from Miss Ellis.

John, she shouted, can you help me? He noted the concern in her voice. It wasn't the normal happy Miss Ellis but a very troubled lady.

What's wrong? he said, running back up the path.

I need you to take the top off my piano, she said. It won't play. Something is wrong and I have a full day of lessons.

Well, calm down and don't panic, said John. We will soon sort that out.

However, that was not to be. A shock awaited them all and a very distraught Miss Ellis just collapsed on the sofa.

John could not believe what he was seeing. All the wires serving the notes had been cut. The piano was useless.

As all the other students for the day arrived with parents keen to drop them off, they were faced with a broken-hearted Miss Ellis.

As they all consoled her, she remembered the door key. A dawn of realisation – someone had indeed entered her property and just purposely sabotaged her piano. But why? Who could ever do such a thing?

As the tears just flowed and all were trying to console her, the story went round and was later well publicised around the town. Even the bus driver made a visit.

The police were called but there was little for them to go on so time was the only healer.

When it became common knowledge about the key in the door it was agreed no burglar was involved. It was purely someone bearing a grudge. But try as they might no one could think who that someone might be.

The people all rallied round, so out of something quite evil the love for Miss Ellis was apparent and again she was overcome – but for a totally different reason.

They collected a sum of money to get the strings renewed and new door locks fitted. In addition, a doorbell fitted with a camera in place. The income she had lost was covered and the lessons restarted.

The discovery of such an evil action did have an advantage. It revealed the amazing bond one lady, only ever known as Miss, had with all around her and how kind people can be with a previously unknown devotion.

Some ten happy years later, Miss Ellis was finishing the washing up when the doorbell rang. She had no lessons on for today so it may be a delivery she thought. Unbeknown to her she was certainly right.

On opening the door she was faced with a very beautiful young lady – in her judgement about twenty years old.

Miss Ellis, the young lady said. You are looking well.

Do I know you, was the pleasantly surprised reply, thinking it could be one of those clever sales visits.

You obviously don't recognise me but I attended your piano lessons many years ago. My name is Sharon, Sharon Marsh.

Oh my God, Sharon, I can see it's you now – come in – come in, said a joyous Miss Ellis.

Sharon joined her in the kitchen as she made a cup of tea.

It's still as cosy as ever in here, she said, and you still have your old piano.

Yes, said Miss Ellis. I have to keep it tuned but it has served me well.

I thought you would have had an electric one by now, said Sharon. They are brilliant – sleek – and don't need tuning.

Can't afford one of those came the reply.

So tell me, Sharon – What are you doing now and what brings you here today – it's been so long.

We all moved up to Manchester where my father worked as a solicitor.

When I left school I moved on to College and then trained as a secretary and have just moved back down here with my partner and now work with Banyons the solicitors in town.

That's marvellous, said Miss Ellis.

Before I answer the second part of your question, said Sharon. If you moved your piano to that corner over there you could get an electric piano a nice distance away from it and the electric point is just there.

That would be nice, said Miss Ellis. But dreams are for the night time.

Well to answer that second part of your question. Guilt brings me here and I have lived with it for many years.

Miss Ellis was totally confused.

When I was a young child I didn't realise what a spoilt little brat I was and surely you must remember that tantrum I had when you kept correcting my order of the fingers, playing the notes.

Yes, chuckled Miss Ellis – I certainly do and you never returned. It happens when you are young but you have matured now to a lovely young lady and it's such a pleasure to see you now. But…. why are you crying?

It was me who cut the strings on your piano, said Sharon. And the guilt has plagued me for many years. So, I have a surprise for you.

While Miss Ellis was trying to come to terms with what she had said, Sharon went to the door and beckoned a crew standing by the gate.

Sitting in shock, Miss Ellis watched helplessly as two men under Sharon's direction moved her old piano over and placed a new electric piano in its place. Plugged it in and switched it on.

Now, said Sharon as the men left. Come up here – and she gently pulled Miss Ellis up and took her to her new piano stool. Would you mind now playing Greensleeves for me, she said.

It was Miss Ellis's turn for the tears to flow as she ran her fingers through the chords of Greensleeves.

There followed a very emotional period between the two of them.

Am I forgiven now? said a tearful, happy and very relieved Sharon.

Story 5

THE GUARDIANS OF LIFE IN 1963

I t was a March day and the windy season, but the sudden onslaught of gales was horrendous. Stronger than Jack Stubbs had ever experienced in all his farming years working in the fields. Today he was lucky. With the skies darkening, he had opted to take his old Fordson Major tractor out for a run. But in reality there really wasn't the need for him to travel out today. All seeds were set and some crops were already showing good growth. His concern in essence was the sugar beet and what stage of growth, if any, it had reached. He was hoping the lines of plants would be clear to see so he could call in the seasonal workers from the village to single the plants out.

A hoeing exercise walking up and down the rows chopping out the surplus and leaving single plants a foot or thereabouts apart. This year the rates would be set at one shilling and three pence per one hundred yards.

It was a lovely field – perfectly flat and level – some twenty-six acres set between thick woodland. The wildlife was plenty and varied. Pheasants and partridges are in abundance this time of year, as are the hares and the rabbits with the breeding season fairly imminent. The Muntjak and the Deer enjoy the safe haven of these remote woods.

There was a lovely footpath from a minor side road about a mile down the hedge line which circled the wood and linked up to the track leading to Jack's Farm. It was well favoured by dog walkers.

Jack stopped the tractor, wet his finger and pointed it in the air outside his cab. It proved the wind direction even though pretty obvious by the movement of the trees. He drove around the headland to the far corner of the wood, finding the calmest spot.

He clambered down and quickly buttoned his coat fully up before venturing across the field. As usual for this field, and to a degree it should be expected, growth was slower extending some forty yards away from the wood. From that point on plants were beginning to appear.

He then walked across and down a few rows – kneeling occasionally to judge sizes and the annoyingly thick groups in places – Indicating some work was needed to get the seed drill settings corrected.

In any event he knew it would be another seven to ten days before action would be needed.

The wind had dropped a bit as he made his way back to the tractor. Glancing across the field he couldn't fail to notice an animal of some description was running towards him. As it got closer, he saw it was a dog. It was running straight for him with purpose, and with some concern he stopped walking and waited for what he feared could be an attempted mauling. It looked like a labrador – it was certainly a big animal.

Maintaining a safe distance, it slowed to a stop and, looking up at Jack, it then turned and swung away. With a breath of relief Jack continued his walk back to his tractor. But the dog came running to him again. Again, it looked up at him and then turned away.

Jack was familiar with animals and started to think something was odd. That thought was proved when the dog turned again but this time came with caution but some purpose and actually grabbed Jack's trousers and pulled before running off again.

Jack knew then that something was wrong as he not only noticed he had a collar but also a lead was in place.

He moved towards the dog, and as soon as he got close the dog ran on another ten to twenty yards. They had reached the edge of the wood when the dog suddenly turned and moved through the hedges, across a ditch and into the area of trees. As it turned and waited, Jack followed through, but when the dog turned to run on again it was suddenly pulled back. Jack soon caught up and cautiously bent down to the animal, watching its eyes carefully. The lead had got firmly stuck – jammed tight between two roots. How ever this hasn't got stuck before, Jack thought, beats me. He carefully took the clip off the collar and freed the dog and then managed to get the lead free. He coiled it up and put it in his coat pocket. The dog was patiently waiting before moving forward again.

Jack stumbled on, cursing to himself as the dog rounded a group of trees and never re-appeared. On rounding the trees, a breathless Jack was in shock. The dog was sitting and licking the head of a small girl who lay lifeless in front of him. When Jack saw her, he turned to be sick. She was only a child. About ten or eleven years old he judged. Her leg was a mass of blood – mangled by a poacher's snare. God knows how long the poor kid had been there. Jack leant down to check her pulse which was faint but there. He then made himself firmly comfortable on the ground and applied his strength to open the snare and free the girl's leg. It was a real mess and the shock and pain must have been horrendous. With both feet now forcing the snare back, ensuring it stayed open, he pulled the girl clear. Once he had pulled her feet clear there was a crack as the snare snapped shut again.

Jack carried the girl out to a flat area in a clearing and laid her gently on the ground. Her leg was in a dreadful state with blood flowing again. He pulled off his coat and then his jacket. He had to do something to prevent even more loss of blood. He searched for his knife and cut the arm off his jacket pulled the girl's boot off and threaded the sleeve up her leg. He took off his belt and lightly tightened it at the top of the leg and used the dog's lead to lightly tighten the sleeve in place lower down and well clear of the damaged area. He then cut the other sleeve off his jacket and used that to tie the girl's legs together. He lifted her onto his coat and wrapped it around her, then carefully stood and lifted her clear.

Urgency and fear now overtook him. For her to have any chance he had to get her to hospital fast.

With great difficulty he managed to get her up with him in the tractor and he started his drive back to the farm but suddenly turned and swung back down the field to the lane at the bottom.

He had remembered today was the doctor's day in the village. Every Wednesday appointments were seen in the village hall. He drove there as fast as he could in his old machine with the dog following close behind.

Sure enough, the doctor's car was there.

He carefully got out of his cab, leaving the girl lying across the seat and ran into the hall. Pushing all aside, he went through to the doctor.

Sorry, Doc, but I have a child barely alive outside – she has lost a lot of blood and is unconscious. He apologised to the half-dressed Mrs Franklin as she clutched her clothes to her bare breasts in shock as he and the doctor ran out to the tractor. Together they lifted the girl down and back onto the table in the doctors' room – with the dog in attendance also.

The doctor immediately rang for an ambulance to be sent urgently and then spoke to the hospital.

Jack relayed exactly how he had found her and what state she was in then.

With the immediate need for a blood transfusion, the doctor could only test her blood and relayed the information of the blood type straight back to the hospital.

It was the actions of a devoted animal together with human understanding that led to the young girl's life happily being saved.

Two days later the girl's parents arrived at the farm. Jilly is recovering now thanks to you, they said. It will take many weeks but we – and she – can't thank you enough. Any time you need help or anything please contact us. We live at the old vicarage.

Oh, and Tinker wants to say thank you too.

With that the golden labrador jumped up to Jack with tail wagging fiercely. After two licks he was pulled away and with a wave and a blown kiss from the lady they left.

Some twenty years later his close friend and housekeeper Jackie dropped by. I have taken the liberty, she said, of buying you a ticket to the Carlton Music Show. Whilst an isolated old monk, I am sure you listen to music.

Not so much of the old, said Jack, and you flipping well know music is my passion.

That's settled then, said Jackie. There are a group of us going so we will pick you up – seven o'clock on Saturday. Do you think you can be ready? she said with a sly smirk.

Jack turned her around and pushed her to the door.

Saturday arrived and Jack certainly was ready, looking strangely like an old Beatle. On arrival he was quite shocked to be ushered with them all to the front row.

Several acts played and it was the most enjoyable show Jack had ever been to – but more was yet to come. The star of the show was on next and indeed it was to be the final act. So Scarlett Rose came on to a rousing round of applause supported by her group known as 'The Pigtails'. They soon got underway with their first song with Scarlett getting the whole house going.

She finished the second number – then the third – then stopped for a break.

She moved a stool across and looked around the theatre. I thank you all, she said, and I mean that most sincerely. This is the most beautiful place I have ever performed in and for me holds a special memory. Many years ago I lived in the village of Midcroft, not far from this city, but we moved away when I was very young. I had a close companion there – a right Tinker. One day I was out for a walk with Tinker – in fact I always had to take him for a walk – but on this day he was my guardian angel as I got caught in a trap. Being my guardian angel, he led my saviour to me. That man was Jack Stubbs and I'd like to invite him to join me now on stage.

Jack was in complete shock as Jackie helped him up and moved him up the steps to the stage where Jilly (stage name Scarlett) took over with an embrace to buffer his tears – tears of pride, love and happiness.

She released him and proceeded to let the world know.

Jack, she said. We have never met since. I know what ordeal you went through in saving my life. My parents moved to South Africa having delayed the move until I was released from care, but the whole event was relayed to me. There was a detailed police report following your being interviewed by them, and the medical and press reports, and I have always kept them. The older I got the more I vowed I would find you and today for me is the best day ever of my life.

She turned to the audience. Tinker was my dog. My loyal friend. I got caught in a snare in the woods, passed out with the shock and pain whilst being very close to bleeding to death. Tinker ran off and found Jack here and made him follow and find me. My ambulance was a tractor but, Jack, when you get home you will find a new tractor waiting for you. You are a lovely man, and this is also for you – my last picture of Tinker.

With that she gave him a kiss and moved him to the steps – whispering in his ear I will be seeing you later. Then sang down to him 'we've met again'. Her modified version of the old Vera Lynn song loved by all.

Story 6

JAKE'S PROGRESS

W hy is it the oldies never understand? Were they never young once?

It never ceases to amaze me how everybody with wrinkles knows all the answers to life. They don't try to understand the use of computers hence reject them. They don't like mobile phones and only use them with constant moans but they are the wise ones. Any queries I may have with problems at school are answered with so much wisdom and always my fault. Always my lack of something or other.

Charlie Haslop was venting his feelings to his older sister Mary.

Mary had been sitting quietly by her desk – halfway through writing a letter to her boyfriend when Charlie had suddenly burst in.

Have you finished your rant, Charlie? she said hopefully but with some restraint

Well the only person who always listens and helps me is old Jake up the road, he replied. He is patient – he asks all the right questions – he then offers his opinion. It is not a 'Thou shalt' – It is a 'have you considered this' – 'have you considered that' before ultimately making the statement –

for whatever it is worth my opinion is this or my advice would be that.

Whilst Mum and Dad, our parental guides, were relaxed with a cuppa and totally absorbed watching Emmerdale, I gave up, grabbed my coat and quietly left – I needed to see Jake but noticed your light was on. I have got it off my chest now, so thank you for that.

Before Mary could say anything, Charlie left. Mary shook her head and turned to her letter, hearing the front door slam and a shout from her father.

Once again the peace of the Haslop household had been Charlied.

It was quite a pleasant evening and Blackberry Lane was quiet. With no traffic movement, Charlie's vision of bitterness was still of his parents. They were always absorbed in their watching of Emmerdale or some other soap and settled in their own confident worlds. Never a moment to listen to the modern world to learn something themselves while giving their advice from their understandings. That bitterness faded with the walk and on arrival at Jake's gate a more stable temperament existed.

As normal Jake twisted round to look through his lounge window and as usual was met with a beaming smile as he carefully got up to come and let Charlie in.

It was one of those rare happenings in life where a close association of love and trust is formed. Charlie was ten years old and running home from school when he tripped and fell badly just outside Jake's house. He was in the garden and had heard the scream and his crying out with the pain. He ran out and tried to lift Charlie onto his feet but saw how serious it was and carried him into his house. Both knees were quite badly grazed and very painful, but he cleaned them up, quietly telling Charlie to calm down. With each knee carefully bandaged and other minor issues dealt with, he kept Charlie in the warmth until his parents came home. That was the start of a true friendship which developed further when Jake himself was taken ill. At fourteen Charlie took charge of his house and looked after Jake's close ally – the golden retriever dog, Dana. A beautiful creature – they were so close and his return from hospital had been wonderful to witness – a magical reunion.

Sadly, Dana had to be put down to release her from the constant pain of an incurable illness, and both Jake and Charlie were in mourning for weeks – neither of them would ever forget her.

So Charlie – you can put the kettle on, said Jake but what brings you round this time of the day?

I just needed to get away from disinterested people and get with someone who listens to me, said Charlie.

Now you have got me thinking, said Jake. By the way I have been offered a young puppy.

I hope it's not one of those yappy little terriers, Charlie replied as he stirred the tea and removed the tea bags.

There is only one breed for you and me, said Jake – it's a golden retriever.

Charlie was in shock but very happy with the thought of a new Dana.

Anyway, said Jake. Let's hear what your problem is today. And to avoid a second problem remember mine is two sugars.

And stirred anti-clockwise, I mumbled.

When is the new canine due, I said – as I took my place on the sofa – and I hope it's a bitch.

Probably another two weeks, said Jake, but yes, it is a bitch. Anyway – your problem of the day – give me my new challenge.

To be honest, Jake, it will be difficult for you to understand but I know you will take an interest… unlike others I could mention.

Come on, said Jake – cast past issues aside, you are with me now so start my new test.

This will be a tester for you, Jake, Charlie remarked. Forgive me for saying this but the computer age we live in now is a new era. I cannot expect you to understand but with the greatest of respect to you – you always listen.

You might be surprised, said Jake. As I sit here vegetating day by day and with no Dana for company I do a lot of reading. Remember you introduced me to a mobile and then a tablet. With your early tuition and my interest leading to reading, trial and discovery you could be surprised.

Charlie glowed with respect for his old friend and ally and so continued.

As stated, Jake, we live now in an internet dominated world gradually controlling our lives. But now there is a new advancement which is both brilliant but in the wrong power crazed and greedy hands quite frightening.

It's AI – that stands for Artificial Intelligence – and believe me it is quite frightening what it can lead to. It can end up controlling everything as it dominates whatever we try and do on our computers – unless we find ways to shut it out. And this is it in its early stages of development. Heaven help us all when it completely takes over.

So – working towards my A levels at school we have been given the task as individuals to put forward a completely new concept for AI to develop. I was looking for ideas and stupidly thinking there would be something from the old days my parents would like to see modernised.

Now you are back on that bitterness trail again, Charlie, so rise above it, said Jake. I will give that some thought.

Have you any ideas yourself?

Yes, but looking for alternatives as my ideas will be laughed at and considered totally stupid.

Well, come on, said Jake. What are they? Let's discuss what you are thinking.

You will think I am mad, said Charlie, but consider the progressions through time. The invention – the advancement.

We advanced through from the Palaeolithic times to the neolithic and then onto the Iron Age.

Then the Agricultural revolution into the industrial revolution.

We must now be in the heart of the digital revolution with the internet and mobile phones and all other communications taking over our lives.

The next generations will be totally controlled – like zombies I fear.

I certainly can't argue with that, said Jake. My fear has been the effects to flight. Will pilots have the skill to fly a plane should their internet control fail?

Now this is where you will think I am totally stupid, said Charlie.

I was struggling to find something new – something relative to our modern day but something that would revolutionise something and bring advantage.

Nothing would come to mind.

But then a series of home events gave rise to an idea.

My father had set up a chicken run. Much against Mother's objections. The mess in the garden was amplified but fresh eggs were a blessing.

One summer's day I went to collect the eggs and one bird was on the nest still and suffering from the heat but quite noticeably recovered once the egg was laid and down in the run. Then with winter and the exceptional cold frosts I feared they would suffer from the cold so I checked on the web. It clearly stated that chickens have complete control of their temperature – obviously to a certain degree – via their feathers.

So, returning to my needs for something new on AI.

Fashion came to mind.

The clothing changes over the years through the likes of the agricultural and the industrial revolutions. From the sackcloth to the Victorians to the teddy boys and now the madness era we are in now.

The absolutely crazy new way out fashion parades. They are ludicrous.

So, my mind has drifted back to the chickens – onto animals and birds. Realising then that humans are the only ones that keep changing their clothes. So, my thoughts are now centred on how to develop a new dress code.

Am I mad?

Jake was quiet.

Actually, he said. Your observations are good. No notice is taken of the clothing of anything other than what we humans wear so you have observed a good point. Exactly how that can be applied to us is beyond me, so sorry I just cannot help you with that one. A good observation though I must admit, and indeed food for thought.

As was expected – that food for thought was quickly dispensed with at the school and quickly advanced into a comedy hour.

Many years later Charlie had passed his A levels and was granted a place at the University of Medicine in Aberdeen where he gained his Bsc in Medical Sciences. The results of his studies took him to America with Biomedical studies focusing fully on the human body – its systems and organs.

But in the back of his mind there was its use in fashion combining comparisons with human dress and our feathered friends. With the realisation that hearing aids had moved from just sitting on the ears to being drilled into the skull as a titanium implant made him wonder about feathers – were they a similar activator?

And so the study turned to the veterinary side.

For Charlie life took a cold shower. His original notion, which had bugged him for years, that humans could revolutionise fashion by copying the birds flew completely out of the window. He had never looked into bird biology but discovering now that with one small chicken having over eight thousand feathers comprising four types layered, he deserved the ridicule he suffered at school.

However, with stubborn resolve he decided to study his original idea further. His purpose and determination now was to overcome his initial failure and come up with a sensible solution. A product that could be a sensation throughout.

His ambition now was to become the Musk of the fashion world.

But the second shock came when investigating the fashion industry itself. He found that it was common knowledge the need to have four layers of clothing in place for the winter period. Then it was realised those layers were four separate sets of clothing.

Now a complete new thought process was needed.

The plane was circling London Heathrow. Christmas and the family beckoned.

Seat belts on, a smooth landing and an easy run through customs yielded a relaxing return to the UK for a very tired Charlie.

A very excited Mary was there to meet him and her sisterly hug soon woke him up and all the excitement of being home again took over.

Mum and Dad still watching Emmerdale, I presume? said Charlie.

EastEnders and Coronation Street too, chuckled Mary. But they are well and excited to see you. Also – I bumped into old Jake yesterday. He was taking his dog for its daily run and he asked how you were. I told him you were well and I was picking you up from the airport in the morning. My God, I have never seen anyone so excited. He seemed to suddenly look ten years younger.

I love Jake, Charlie said – in the nicest possible way of course.

He certainly must have missed you – even the dog seemed to know, said Mary.

It was a wonderful homecoming. The telly was off for once but, no doubt everything was set on record.

After things had settled down – can you do me a favour? his father said. When you go down to see old Jake again, please don't slam the door. We have already renewed the hinges once.

There was laughter all round and the night was relaxed with so much to catch up on and a few bevvies in between.

The next day was bright and sunny. Almost as if the heavens knew that Charlie was retracing the steps of his youth, and an even greater reunion was in store.

He walked up the path and tapped the window – some traditions never die.

Jake turned with a broad grin and tears in his eyes. On opening the door the welcome was twofold. Crazy leaps and licks from Dana2 with Jake just hugging so hard with tears flowing. Their bond was amazing.

Once things settled down, with Dana2 on Charlie's lap and Jake asking all the questions, it was clear to see that despite his age he was still the same old Jake. Keen to listen to his Charlie and needing to know about life in America – how his learning and achievements had progressed and what his intentions were now.

As Charlie revealed what he considered to be of interest he returned to their meeting in the past on the AI matter, stating that his latest efforts on his theory had also failed.

But then came the surprise that was to change his life.

Now you remember I said I could only think about it, said Jake. It was one of those times I couldn't help you and it got to me. I just could not let it go with the feeling I had let you down. So, I read and I read. I went to the computer shop and found a boffin. As a result, I have made progress. It doesn't meet what you were originally thinking because to develop that same coating concept as a bird would involve connections into the body. It's all too early for that. But I had a different idea. Now follow me and see what you think.

They moved into the utility room where Charlie was surprised to see a tailor's dummy standing by the window. It was modelling what appeared to be a pullover.

Well – what do you think? said Jake.

Err it's a nice dummy seemingly keeping warm, said Charlie completely confused.

Jake had moved close to the dummy.

And what do you think now? he said.

Charlie was in shock – the model transformed.

And now, said Jake, as it transformed again.

Charlie was stunned. Just how have you done that? he said.

Well after a lot of thought and a lot of reading I realised it was impossible to follow all that you had in mind BUT certainly some changes in a layered style of fashion could be applied.

I then looked into solar energy and worked on a very small needle with a very fine flexible set of small solar panels woven in with the cloth. That was very hit and miss and totally unreliable.

However, fine wires were adopted but in vertical formation on each strip of cloth with delicate switch mechanisms along that thin base girdle. All powered in that girdle by those small but longstanding powerful round batteries used in clocks and doorbells.

You were looking at horizontal layers of feathers with your concept, but I then suddenly realised that for humans they needed to be vertical.

So with a lot of outside help, I devised a method of applying layered clothing with a simple touch control to swing the 25mm wide vertical layers from left to right. Hence the colour change – and hence a new fashion.

But won't the outside help be grabbing your wonderful idea.

No, said Jake. I did it as a garden curtain in a shed to start with and then moved to different people for each phase, so no one knows the result.

That is phenomenal, said Charlie as the tears now flowed down his face.He moved across and gave Jake yet another big hug and suffered more excitement from Dana2.

Charlie finalised his affairs in America and moved back to the UK.

Together with Jake they hired a small workshop and office. Developed that and advanced it to larger premises with employees to start the manufacturing process.

It is now a recognised brand known worldwide as 'Jake's Progress'.

Charlie had great joy in returning to his old school for the 'old boys reunion dinner' carrying a plaque for them to mount.

It stated – 'Jake's Progress from Charlie's schooldays 2025'.

The old boys then had a young moment with memories returning and the old sniggers replaced by new giggles – from the masters also.

Story 7

POLES APART IN 1965

The maximum speed I could get out of my Aerial Golden Arrow was barely 70mph – with a back wind – but it got me the six miles to work and back daily. It was a lovely looking machine and fancied by many with very envious eyes. Having worked with the Post Office telephones some ten months now it was the time for further training so it's now off to the Bletchley Park training school.

It was to get the first qualification to work on overhead lines.

We all signed in – were shown to out dormitories and introduced to our tutor Bill Hughes along with his support staff.

Getting to know the lads was fine and the first evening out down the town very enjoyable, but it soon became obvious that with the various characters you always get one loon.

He was Denis Ellicrank – where such a surname came from no-one dare ask. Before the first week was out the Crank part would be emphasised.

Every day he was chirping away. Giggling at this and guffawing at that. Twice in one lesson Bill Hughes went to his desk and threatened to have him gagged.

It was the time now to work on the actual practical applications on the field side.

So, the field work training was centred upon pole work.

It started with selecting the type of pole to be used – size and height needs.

The testing process applied to poles that had been erected for some time with probes pushed in and out of the woodwork to determine if any degree of wood decay was occurring.

Denis certainly became very annoying on this part with pretending to accidentally prick those close by. He was soon subject to a discipline lecture from the tutor with the dangers of such stupid actions made perfectly clear.

It was then a case of selecting the cross members for carrying the wires and fitting the insulators properly spaced. With the arms fitted, the side struts were bolted in place.

Then down from those arms the steps properly spaced offset on opposite sides.

Denis enjoyed himself with the steps, bolting one in place the wrong way up and once again the subject of a sharp talking to from the trainer.

That left the excavation work then to produce the hole and then the actual pole erection.

With the pole now ready – one per two-man team – the place to be erected chosen and agreed. Then the hole dug.

Denis again had to be shouted at but this time by the neighbouring crew.

Look, you little bastard, said Clive Bentley. You throw one more lump of your mud across and down our hole and you will be buried and backfilled. Got it, you little pile of dung?

There was a chuckle along the line, and the trainers just shook their heads whilst suppressing glances amongst themselves and some turning to have a quiet chuckle.

That was a different phase of learning as it was not just a hole.

First a trench around one metre in length stepped down to finalise with the depth of hole.

The pole itself is carefully slid into the hole with ropes off each side to pull it up and let slowly drop to the bottom of the hole. The hole is then backfilled with the spirit level keeping it upright and making sure the top arms are set in the right direction.

Then it's the personal tuition in use of firstly the safety belt and then the access ladder up to the stepping rungs at the top.

Now each of you once you have passed this course – with the exception of Denis of course – will be working alone, stated Bill Hughes.

Now settle down, lads – it wasn't that funny – it's always sad to see one fail a course.

Oh chuckle chuckle, muttered Denis as his partner for the pole erection duty poked him in the ribs.

Now over here, Denis, said Bill Hughes. This is your safety belt. It is quite easy to put on as Denis will now be shown and he will then demonstrate. It will give you all the confidence of knowing that if Denis can do it – anyone can do it.

A ripple of laughter followed with Bill also having a smug smile beside quite a red-faced Denis.

Now remove the belt which I am showing you now in the hope that when each pole is up you will each remember the belt up procedure.

Each team then turned and erected their poles. Quite an easy and simple process by the method shown. Pole sat at an angle into the trench with a rope at the top set up in two lengths. With the two men spaced apart and gently pulling back on the ropes, the pole is easily erected. Trench backfilled –complete area tamped hard with upright checked and the land reinstated.

Now, said Bill Hughes. The next phase is the ladder. You will be working alone in the field so that ladder needs to be safe. You must have this rope firmly tied on the top rung. Raise the ladder up to a safe height to comfortably move from the ladder you have climbed onto the first step of your pole.

You run the rope then down the rungs on the right side and out at hip height, twist it around so it is now on the outside like this, then raise the ladder and extend it up your pole to your selected safe height.

Take the rope then around the pole and return it to the left side of the ladder pulling it tight and tying it off like this. As you can now see whatever force you use you cannot push that ladder over.

So now for your point of action. Will those elected to climb their pole first now put on their safety belts.

Bill went round and checked them all.

Now, he said – walk to your pole and stand beside it. Now bring your belt around the pole and fasten it as I showed you firmly back on itself.

He waited while they all completed that action then walked around checking them all.

Now, he said – when I give the word, all lean straight back keeping your feet close to the pole and you will be held firm at forty-five degrees away from the pole and free to work safely with both hands. That is all of you of course except that village idiot Denis who will fall over backwards having deliberately prepared to be the centre of attention. So come on, Denis, put your belt on correctly.

Again once the giggles and sniggers had died down everything went smoothly. The procedure was repeated several times, making sure all were fully familiar and in time it would be a process completed as second nature.

Now, said Bill, to complete this morning's work each team will erect and make safe their ladders. I will check those before letting you climb, you then move up onto your steps and then climb up to a comfortable working position. You will then have made your belt safe and secure around the pole to lean back on for comfortable working.

So now onwards and upwards. And then we stop for lunch.

The exercise went well. There were moments noted where to lean back some clung to the pole but eventually gained the confidence to overcome their fear and settled back waving arms to all.

That's great, said Bill. You can all come down now. It's lunchtime so see you all back here at 1.30. He turned and left.

He didn't hear the call from Denis – or if he did, he ignored it. As did all the teams as they left for their lunch with Denis hollering his head off to get him down.

The neighbouring team with a nod to Denis's partner had quietly untied his ladder and taken it down. All were looking forward to a peaceful lunchbreak.

It was a lovely sunny day so Jimmy Buckle and Freddie Level decided to take their ice cream and bottle of squash over to the work area. The noises began as they approached. A very sad Denis squealing out pleas to help him down. As Jimmy and Freddie sat in the grass close by, others came to join them.

Can you hear those funny noises? they said.

I think it's a child's playground from the infant school, said Gerry.

Please, said Denis – I need the toilet.

Can you smell anything strange, said Tommy – Hmm, they said – a bit like dogs' poo.

They left it a while longer as the time was marching on before quietly moving across and restoring the Denis ladder. I still keep hearing that funny noise, they said, but let's move away from that smell.

A very sullen Denis clambered painfully down and walked very gingerly across to his room.

Five minutes later, Bill Hughes was back and ready to give the team their final brief on how to install a stay.

First how to make up the wire and fix it high up on their pole and then selecting the distance for the hole dig. Firstly, install and then learn the method of tensioning and fixing the wire.

Now it seems we are one short. That prat Denis.

Anyone know where he is?

Yes, Bill, said Jimmy Buckle – he had to return to his room to change his nappy.

Story 8

NEVER NEVER LAND

When you work away from home a lot, any opportunity of taking your better half with you is always grabbed. Not always agreed – but always offered.

We had travelled to the Isle of Wicks. A beautiful island off the northern coast and one very close to the heart of Patricia – my wife – as she originated from the North. The south attraction being the advancement with education – so a must for her– and accepted with both fervour and excitement.

We met at university. A feisty young lady. Good fun – great wit with terrific energy – BUT – upset her and you need to take cover.

On the other hand, I was the opposite – taking most things in my stride with no sensitive reactions. Just as well really, as my name – Jimmy Choo – became the focus of her humour imitating a steam train when introducing me in parties or other gatherings.

Whilst being pure English – my mother had met and ultimately married Zhai Choo and hence Choo became the family name; but now the Patricia jokes would stop as with our marriage Patricia Lonsdale became Mrs Patricia Choo. The jokes then transferred across to her when at reunions with friends as the intro started with sneezing and the shouting of Trischoo Trischoo!

With all the survey work finished and flight booked earlier, it was time to travel to the airport. It was a clear fine day with the sun breaking through. We arrived in good time and parked the hire car back in the returns bay. We would advise and return the keys at the desk once our flight was booked in.

On the one hand we were then lucky for not handing in the car keys but on the other hand devastated to be told our flight had been taken over by the football club flying out for a cup match.

We would be firmly booked on the next flight tomorrow afternoon.

Quite dejected, we collected the car and just sat there wondering what to do. A hotel is the first need, I said, but I don't want to go back into the town.

No, said Tricia. There was a hotel that I saw when we drove in. It's beside those funny bunds and close to the sea. We could try there.

Ok, I said – and started the car. The short journey was done in complete silence but then the bunds revealed themselves to be a historic ancient domain or burial ground. They perked up as Jimmy suggested they check if the hotel has any vacancy – book in – and then relax, discovering the mysterious bunds and taking a walk along the beach. For two people always on the go, this sudden downward change in energy and purpose was difficult to come to terms with.

The hotel was quiet with rooms available. Jimmy made the booking, and they took their bags up to a nice double bedroom overlooking the sea through a very large bay window. Well satisfied, they thanked the lady at reception – who seemed to be covering all duties – and returned to the pre-historic area for discovery.

Nice hotel, said Trish. Quiet with a lovely view.

I agree, said Jimmy, but there is something odd about it.

Why do you say that? said Trish.

Well didn't you notice the other rooms on the way up to our room? said Jimmy. They all had huge padlocks in place.

Can't say I did, said Trisha. It's just security, I guess.

Not with a great bar across and a padlock the size of my fist, said Jimmy. It's weird and I felt the lady serving us was a bit on edge.

It's one night so just stop worrying about it. Apply your vivid imaginations to those bunds.

Jimmy shrugged his shoulders and began the mystery tour.

Having had a brief walk along the beach the pair remained in a quiet mood. Both were fed up with the way events had gone. They returned to the hotel and after a visit to their room decided to visit the bar.

It was there that things got worse.

There was a young group of quite rough looking guys sitting on the far side of the bar. They just stared at the new entrants.

The young lady serving looked very nervous.

I'll have a pint of bitter please, said Jimmy.

Have you made your mind up yet, Trisha? he said.

Make mine a half of lager, she replied.

Then it started.

Oh a half of lager – came the shout putting on a posh accent.

Oh mine too, said another.

Trisha looked furious. The bar lady was shaking. Aren't you going to say something? she said – looking up at Jimmy.

Leave it, he said.

The banter went on and Trisha had to be ushered away from the bar and forced by Jimmy to take their drink up to their room.

Trisha was furious. You are a coward; she shouted at Jimmy. I really do not believe it. You stood back and did nothing.

Listen said Jimmy. That is exactly what they wanted. They would have killed us both. Young – fit – obviously hate interlopers and were determined to get rid of us. There is something about this place. Never known such tension.

Trisha never spoke and a very quiet evening was spent locked in their room.

It was 2am when Jimmy awoke. Lights were flashing outside it seemed. He went to the window. There were two Land Rovers on the beach but then a flash of light from out to sea.

Repeated from one of the Land Rovers below.

He turned and woke Trisha. Quick, he said, and keep the light out.

She stumbled half-awake to the window behind Jimmy.

Look below and wait, he said.

My God, she said, they are signalling to a boat out at sea.

And that is precisely why they wanted us out, said Jimmy. They are drug dealers and a violent lot who will stop at nothing with the stakes involved.

We really should get out of here.

Trisha grabbed Jimmy's arm and pulled him round with a finger on her lips. She then pointed to the door.

They crept over and could hear what was probably the padlock being removed from the door into the next door room.

They carefully crept back and sat quietly on the bed.

I am sorry, Jimmy, Trisha whispered. You recognised a serious situation. I know now that we could be in serious danger.

We daren't try and leave now, said Jimmy. They would kill us both with what they have at stake. We must keep quiet, sit it out and hope they have gone by morning. Then we can just leave quietly.

They decided to keep away from the windows and try and just get some sleep. By keeping quiet it was hoped all would be safe and so a very restless night was endured.

All was as they had desperately hoped – very quiet in the morning. The place was cold, empty – totally deserted. Then the nervous one appeared and offered breakfast, but

Jimmy and Trisha just paid their bill and left. They were keen to get away and neither ever wanted to return to this Island. However, things were about to take a serious turn for the worse.

With cases thrown on the back seat they breathed a sigh of relief – gave each other a knowing look and carefully backed out of the hotel car park. It was only a few miles to the airport so there was no hurry. Jimmy turned to put the radio on when Trisha screamed. That scream was followed by a big bang as a pickup truck rounding the bend at speed had apparently lost control and smashed into them.

Trisha was shaken and bruised but Jimmy was silent. She grabbed his arm and gently shook it but there was no response. Jimmy, she screamed and forced open the passenger door running round to the driver's side. Other drivers had stopped and had run over to help. They were able to get the smashed door open when the police arrived. They were quickly followed by an ambulance. With the usual calm organisation, the police and the ambulance crew got Jimmy carefully lifted clear and stretchered into the ambulance. Trisha joined him, leaving the police to deal with all the control and the recovery of their hire vehicle.

As usual, the emergency services were focussed and thorough. The good news was that Jimmy had recovered consciousness and was considered out of danger, but a full brain and body check was programmed and in progress. Trisha had been very fortunate and apart from the shock and some bruising had been checked thoroughly and set up quietly in a side ward with calming sedatives whilst waiting for news on Jimmy.

The police had arrived and were in deep conversation with a member of the medical staff.

With the prescribed medication calming and relaxing her and with reports given that Jimmy was in no danger, Trisha slipped into a deep sleep.

It was nine o'clock that morning the accident had happened. It was now nightfall. Trisha stirred but was given more fluid and told to just relax and get some sleep. Considering the lack of any sleep with the events of the night before, and with the knowledge both she and her Jimmy were ok and in safe hands, she did as she was told and returned to slumber.

The next morning Trisha woke with a start to the sound of a trolley. It was the breakfast trolley. A very serious lady who didn't seem to speak much English served a tea and offered her porridge. With little response from the lady, Trisha clambered off the bed and moved to the door. As she peered out looking to see who she could call, a stern voice said – Please Miss, stay by your bed. A nurse will come to you in due course.

Trish was in shock – why are you guarding my door? she said. It was an accident that was not of our making. We are the ones who have suffered and we have nowhere to go. I want my husband. I want to get out of here – away from this place – away from this horrible island. With that she completely broke down and collapsed to the floor.

Jimmy was in some discomfort but sitting beside his bed in a neighbouring isolation ward when he heard Trisha screaming out words of desperation. He gingerly got up and hobbled slowly to the door but he too was stopped by a policeman seemingly on guard.

As the man got up, ushering with his arms to Jimmy to get back and stay in his room, Jimmy gesticulated and protested with some frustrated but controlled anger.

But it's my wife, said a desperate Jimmy. I need to get to her.

The nurses are with her now, Sir, the policeman replied.

So what is going on? said Jimmy. Why are you here? We are not criminals – it was an accident and not caused by us. We were on our way to the airport and should have gone yesterday but your damn footballers grabbed our seats.

Don't worry, Sir, it will all be clearly set out for you soon enough.

Jimmy turned and went back to his chair but saw in so doing the emergency button which he duly pressed.

A nurse appeared very quickly.

Now what is going on? said Jimmy. How is my wife – I heard her screaming? How bad was she hurt?

She is fine, said the nurse. It is just the trauma and reactions coming out.

And what is my problem? said Jimmy.

I guess you may have a headache as you were concussed but no other brain injury was sustained. You have heavy bruising and a cracked rib – all on your right side, but you will be released with your wife later today I am sure.

As she turned to leave, Jimmy said – but why are the police here?

The nurse just looked at him and said, don't worry they will take care of you.

With that and a very strange look she left.

The two were in shock as on discharge they were swiftly taken to a police van, driven to the Police station, cautioned and placed in separate cells. Neither knew the reasons why they were being so humiliated and were each now in even greater shock.

After two hours glumly pacing the cell, Jimmy was taken to an interview room where two officers sat ready to question him.

This is Detective Constable Morrison and I am Detective Inspector Phillips.

We understand you were travelling towards the airport when you were hit by an oncoming vehicle. Your situation was very fortunate for us hence you have since been cautioned.

Jimmy then spoke up.

Why was our accident so fortunate for you? That's madness.

DI Philipps ignored the outburst and pointed to some bags standing in the corner of the room.

Are those your bags, Sir? he asked quite sternly.

Those two are but that one isn't, said Jimmy.

Are you sure about that, Sir? the DI said.

You think I don't know our own bags? replied Jimmy angrily.

Calm down, Sir, said the DI. How come that isn't your bag. It was in your car.

Listen, said Jimmy, I came to this island to work.

And where was that, Sir? asked the DI.

At the Shell site down by the harbour, said Jimmy

I took the opportunity to bring my wife with me. We were robbed of our seats on the plane yesterday by your damn football team and were forced to stay overnight. That bag is not ours.

Strange that, Sir – it seems it was hidden in the boot of your car.

For a start, said Jimmy, that is not our car, it is obviously a hire car. We were on our way to return it at the airport and bloody well fly out of this place, he said sarcastically. Besides, we have never been able to access the boot. Our bags were on the back seat.

The DI went quiet, looked down and then glancing across to his colleague announced the interview was suspended at 1530 hours and returned a very angry Jimmy to his cell.

They called Trisha in and repeated the same line of questioning. Then were quite surprised to receive almost identical answers.

Again the interview was suspended and Trisha was returned to her cell.

DI Phillips and DC Morrison were not happy.

There is something wrong here, said the DI.

I completely agree, said DC Morrison, but can't put my finger on it. They approached Superintendent Higgins and relayed the events.

Have you checked on his work claims? said the superintendent.

Yes, they confirm he has worked on their site for a full week. Was diligent and they have set him a return date in two months' time for a maintenance check to keep the HSE happy.

So he is a responsible citizen in reality and not likely to be our man.

I think you need to get both of them together and question them carefully and softly – it looks very much as though they have been innocent victims. Carriers with no knowledge on a hire vehicle with a secured boot.

Bring them in here.

Both Jimmy and Trisha shed a tear as they met up again and were allowed to hold hands as they were led into Superintendent Higgins' office.

He introduced himself whilst the DI and the DC sat quietly to the side watching the expressions unfold with Jimmy and Trisha.

You may think this unusual suddenly being brought into the office of senior management but together – the Di, the Dc and myself – think something is amiss and we just need to clarify matters before moving forward.

I will let you know some background with regards to how you have ended up in your position, if you could first relay to me why when your work was completed that you couldn't leave and events on from there.

Jimmy was about to explode but Trisha turned and told him to calm down. Leave it to me, please Jimmy, she said. I think I can see why we have had to suffer and we cannot blame these people.

She went on to quietly relay the events from the booking cancellation at the airport, to finding the hotel and then the set of events that they suffered within that hotel. As she moved onto the accident the tears flowed and Jimmy just hugged her tightly to him.

All three officers were in shock. A case they had been investigating for a year or more looked to be solved by a wrongful arrest and the pair's earlier sufferings.

My God, said the Superintendent, we can only apologise for the treatment you have received and your earlier sufferings. We will make every effort now to make it up to you.

The situation is this. We have been investigating for over a year now a drug cartel. They are an evil, violent lot, but we have been unable to pin them down. It seems to me your walking away from that 'half a lager' jibe actually saved you. You could have been dumped at sea and both washed back ashore by now.

We will keep watch on that place and wait for the two Land Rovers to return. With that special lock on the boot of that hire car that company is obviously involved. They must have seen the car and rang their accomplice. He probably told them not to be concerned as you were flying out hence you were left alone. And they used you as the courier back to that evil hire company.

The relief and understanding with Jimmy and Trisha was obvious to all.

Now, said the superintendent. It is up to us now to make amends so get yourselves a shower and change of clothes. The canteen will give you a special and I will arrange your flight home. How does that sound?

The relief shown by Jimmy and Trisha was a treat for all to see.

The Super certainly kept his word. The DI and the DC took their bags to their unmarked car and drove them out to a helipad. With firm handshakes, thanks and apologies, the two were settled in the police helicopter and delivered to a point very close to their home back in the UK.

It was a month later that the news headlines reported of the success of the island police in smashing a drugs ring with a link also into a lucrative people smuggling racket.

Trisha turned to Jimmy as they sat watching the news. So our twin pain was the country's gain, she said. But I will certainly be thinking twice before travelling with you again.

Story 9

TIMED OUT

L iving in the spirit of things is now completely different. It is a reality.

When I left my human body, I became aware. The loss to me was turning into an adventure so unique, so unbelievable, but with returning back to control a dawning of light shone through. My thoughts drifted to the pain for those left behind but they would follow. Then they also would understand.

Arrival was in that ghost format studied by many in that previous life. I understand now that puts those returning into a gradual frame of understanding and drifts them back to their original form but with the continuance of the ultimate purpose.

This new experience had a light shining all around me as a tender voice made me welcome.

You have returned, the voice said. Your duties as a human fulfilled. Are you ready for the next phase?

Yes, I replied – but may I ask – can you enlighten me – I need to understand...

Of course – the voice replied. It will take time for your full understanding to return.

You have been released from our experimental planet called Earth where you have been a very small part of its development. We split it into different areas – different countries – different languages – different beliefs and so on. You were sent this time in the basic human form. Others are there in many different forms recognised as animals, insects, birds, fish and so on.

You will have a choice next as to how you return. Remember our purpose is to ultimately create a planet where we can all settle and enjoy forever as the headquarters of our universe.

How can that be, I replied. With so many different creeds, colours, languages, beliefs? With aggression comes violent energy. Then there is love – with tenderness. Pain and fear are dominant factors so how can you or we be creating a perfect world?

The voice replied.

It is a collection of species from every planet on our universe. The purpose agreed by all has been to amalgamate all in one place and let the reactions occur. From those reactions a complete transformation will be made.

Ok, so when do I return and in what form? I said.

The choice is yours, the voice replied.

I had a very big family and a large group of friends on that planet, I said – and you said they would all return and we would all be together again.

Yes, said the voice. But at different intervals of time of course.

So – a gathering is the need for me, I replied. Community living in a safe warm area. An ant is intelligent. It does a lot for the earth and provides food for the microbes and other organisms. It's so full of energy that body would suit me. It would be a pleasure to be away from all the hassle you put me through being a human being.

The voice had listened with humour and good understanding.

So, it replied – An ant in Antigua will be our decision then, with all family and friends to follow whenever. A small, warm and very safe island in the seclusion of the Caribbean Sea is our reward to you.

So that will now be arranged the voice said. Antigua it is.

And so things were progressed.

Back on earth a study was ongoing in the Jodrell Bank school of physics and astronomy at Manchester University – in the United Kingdom of Great Britain and Northern Ireland. But this study was taking a serious turn with much concern being shown and verging on panic with senior staff being alerted and the Government being contacted.

Everything pointed to an asteroid now expected to hit Earth with a velocity worse than ever before experienced.

With America alerted, efforts were in progress to scramble with any possible means to knock the beast off course.

Being an ant is certainly different. Luckily I have been made a Queen so I will enjoy a life in excess of thirty years, but my poor workers will only be around for one or two years. It is lovely within our small colony being just a few hundred. Scouts from other colonies have visited and they have thousands living in their communities.

I hope some of the workers soon bring me some food – my store stomach is nearly empty whilst my digestive one is becoming slightly uncomfortable. So time to move up.

Today is another lovely day up on the surface and the vibrations are good.

Long may it continue.

NASA had diverted an asteroid earlier in the year which was supposedly the size of a block of flats using a satellite the size of a minicab to knock the beast off course. It succeeded. And now a new attempt was being progressed.

Jodrell Bank were on standby, recording every move with high tension in the air. They waited and waited then let out a huge gasp as the satellite made contact. The result had definitely knocked the rock off course but was it enough?

Everyone was feverishly working out the course and the drop zone, but fear still reigned.

After a few minutes it became clear. It had been knocked off course and would miss the large cities, but the new course would lead it directly to the Caribbean.

Early warnings were on the airwaves across the world and tension around the areas of Trinidad and Tobago was growing fast.

And then it happened. It felt like an earthquake had occurred in the region and the Caribbean Sea was in tidal wave mode. But Trinidad and Tobago areas became more relaxed.

The news then travelled around the world.

The asteroid had been knocked off course but still crashed to Earth.

At least it had avoided the major cities – but the island of Antigua was now no longer.

So the voice will now be plagued by the spirits of a huge ant population aside from others and the moral of this story is:

Even the Gods can get it wrong sometimes.

Story 10

MAINTAINING LIFE'S INTERESTS (LIVING LIFE)

As I stood by the railings, looking out to sea, the reflections from the moon brought reflections to the mind.

Why is it that when life winds down and age progresses the mind races faster than ever – but only back to those early days of youth and ambitions? So many things seen so clearly now whilst the mind stagnates on the current day with any forward focus stuck in reverse gear.

Having spent many happy years with the simple things in life – flirting with the ladies – darts in the pub. Totally consumed with a great group of friends.

Courtship – marriage – happy family and travel were all in the mix. With my son now in Aussie land and wife now an ex, some form of challenge is certainly needed to avoid any further descent into complete sedation.

Life moves in phases. People find partners. They settle down and increase their flock with a new circle of friends now in similar mode. As age creeps on – the children grow up and eventually they too leave home. Then the process starts all over again but for the new young – leaving our energies left to just focus on reflection. I have got to make a change.

That change came quicker than could ever have been imagined. Having worked in many different areas of the world taught one to always be alert – take stock of everything around you – observe attitudes – avoid knee jerk reactions but be prepared to deal with wrongdoings, but walk away from serious dangers.

It was an innocent observation in a remote village shop that sparked off the plan.

Several weeks passed before the first happening occurred.

Poor old Mr Trent ran a small convenience store. He was no threat to any of the supermarkets but held a good choice on his shelves of the treats loved by the young. Every school day brought a flurry of young scholars in to empty his shelves. It had been noted that is exactly what they did, but few items were indeed paid for.

Visiting the store regularly and meditating around the newspaper and paperback stand rendered my presence insignificant.

But I was noting events and decided that now was the time to leave.

Meanwhile at the end of the shop a concentrated group of young men were busily attending to their needs before turning into a boisterous group of rebels. They became loud and threatening as they prepared now to face an even shakier Mr Trent.

Suddenly the shop door was flung open and then quickly slammed shut with sign turned to closed and blind pulled down. A man fully masked stood there – but no one would be bothered by that mask. A common sight even now with those still fearing Covid.

He moved across to Mr Trent and firmly said – Please, you just stay there. I have some annoying young men to deal with. When I give the word call the police but not before. Understood?

Yes, whispered a confused Mr Trent with fear obvious in his voice.

The man walked purposely down to the left and then yelled.

You lot – Up here ... Now.

With some surprise the five obvious bully boys sauntered up.

Who the hell are you, said the obvious leader as he swaggered forward to take charge of the situation. But shock hit him as the man leapt back adopting a squat position with a handgun drawn and aimed straight at his head.

Now get down. On the floor. All of you, he said menacingly.

They did as they were told immediately and as one. The arrogance and bravery of youth reverted to a wobbly state of fear and subservience.

As the man kicked their legs apart, he yelled for Trent to come round. He pointed the gun at the first lout as he stood back.

Now empty those pockets onto the floor.

Trent was in shock – the amount of the material taken off his shelves was unbelievable.

Now your shirts, NOW! shouted the man.

More followed with paperbacks and pencil sets.

Trent – the man said. You have your mobile so take a picture of what you see.

A shaky Mr Trent fumbled with his mobile and did as he was told. Pictures bound to be blurred by his uncontrollable shaking.

The man pointed to the nearest lad. Now – you get up – and trousers off... He yelled out – I said NOW!

As the trousers came down the number of cigars were revealed with other items strapped to the thigh.

The man turned to Trent – Take another picture of what you now see, then you call the police, he said.

Trent turned and again did as he was told.

Now come back here, Trent, and wait by these lads while I stand by the door to let my colleagues in. As the police siren sounded the arrival, the man lifted the blind, changed the shut sign to open. Unlocked the door and left.

The Wellbell Echo had front page news with a difference this week.

SHOPLIFTERS EXPOSED

The photos showed all.

Mr Trent's General Store was no longer just a General store – it was headline news.

The subject of many new visitors – intrigued to see their local film set.

It was an example for all to see – the seriousness of shoplifting and the knock on effects that could have on pricing.

But who was the mystery man? The police are now investigating. They need to find the man with the gun… Before good turns to evil.

I folded the Wellbell Echo up and dropped it on the table, feeling quite proud of myself. That first little exercise went quite well really – shoplifters beware.

With a new purpose in life, it is time for the consumer suppliers' Robin Hood to prepare for action number two.

Another few weeks passed with the focus set onto which naughty activity to deal with next and how.

But things have a habit of happening when least expected and before any such plans have been developed.

I had written a letter for my son and then realised it was his birthday in two weeks' time and decided I should get him a card.

As well as needing the card, I needed stamps and to get the package airmailed. The local post office was ideal. Aside from being a post office, it was almost a mini supermarket with racks of all types of cards and calendars. A new family had taken it over and were gradually upgrading and modernising the business.

It was a cool day but not unpleasant. I nodded to the man behind the counter and continued to the cards.

Weddings – fifties – sixties – ahh general birthdays for men. Some choice indeed.

As I stood trying to decide whether to go for serious or funny there were suddenly threatening noises coming from the front of the shop. I slowly turned my head and looked quietly across. It was the oddest of situations. A masked man was at the post office counter. He had a gun which was pointed directly at the postmaster. He was demanding the till to be opened and all money put in the bag he had produced.

Without thinking I donned my covid mask and carefully withdrew my pistol from my pocket. It was pure chance that I was wearing the coat my dummy handgun was kept in.

With adrenalin racing I leapt out and shouted at the gunman.

Armed police, I shouted – drop it – now.

The gunman turned in shock and went to turn the gun on me. I yelled – Drop it.

Thankfully he did.

Now kick it across to me.

He duly did.

Now get down and lay on the floor, I shouted. On your stomach. Hands behind back.

I glanced towards the counter man and motioned him out.

Get cable ties, string or a rope, I said – and be quick.

The man returned with a ball of string and proceeded under my instruction to tie the man's hands and then his legs.

Now – I said. Call the police.

As he hesitated, I repeated the instruction again. And more firmly.

But you are the police, he said.

Just do as I say, I replied – I will be at the door to guide them in. This man must be taken away and formally charged.

As I heard the police sirens arriving, I slipped quietly away.

The Wellbell Echo had a field day.

With the front-page report from a confused postmaster making it clear that he was saved by that mystery man.

Another occasion that the police focus becomes more intense on finding the identity of Mr Good as all the real baddies had been dealt with for them.

The Wellbell police station was quiet. A meeting had been called in the Super's office which had the effect of putting all concerned on high alert.

Superintendent Glasswell thanked his seniors for their attendance and then continued with the reasons why the meeting had been called.

We are faced with a really strange situation, he said.

You will all be aware of the shoplifter's incident and then the attempted Post Office robbery.

Both averted by a seemingly good citizen.

I won't beat about the bush. As good as that person may be, we need to find him. We need to have him in here and for his own good we need to strictly caution him.

As good a person that he is, his actions can eventually lead to bloodshed…probably his own.

So – has anyone any ideas as to who this man might be?

There followed an awkward silence.

I thought that might be the case, said Superintendent Glasswell as he continued.

Let us consider the man himself.

He is obviously well enough off to be self-supporting.

He has obviously been subject to some kind of training to act as he does.

He can't be that old to take on such actions – some fitness and fleetness of foot needed.

He is obviously bright and I would say studies situations.

So what will be his next target?

I suggest, Sergeant Boyce – you set your team onto checking local people that have recently completed their time in the armed services. Checking with each service recent retirees.

Sergeant Jones. Alert your crews to situations in the area where there is a pattern of minor thefts or similar. Focus on any you consider could be our ghostly helper's next target. He obviously observes and watches for a while to be accurate in his timing and planning.

If any have luck to come across him, treat with some dignity as he is on the right side. Remember he is armed, but my belief is it is a starter pistol, kids from the cowboys days or even an old real with no bullets. Not something we can say for certain but a probability. He does not give any impression of intentions to harm even the baddies; he uses it simply to take control.

Any questions?

The room was quiet and so with the Super's thanks they all quietly left to set up the new investigations.

After listening to the news and seeing the concerns raised in the newspapers, my next challenge soon became clear. With the shoplifting problem now reaching epidemic proportions, any prevention, however small, was a help. So the time had now come to review the neighbourhood stores, build a picture –and plan.

Sergeant Boyce had no joy finding any military retirees. The MOD were very helpful but there was nothing of any significance other than the aged or the wounded.

As the weeks passed, nothing but blanks had been drawn and tension was mounting with the timing likely to be right for another happening.

As superintendent Glasswell moved around the office, creating an atmosphere of discomfort amongst a group that were already well depressed, Sergeant Jones returned. He was in a jubilant mood which confused all – but that confusion was soon replaced by some sighs of relief.

I was surprised at the lack of people in the 'Gerrard stores' but then realised it was an away game for the town and the main shoppers would either be up the city or home again. I went to the back of the shop and studied the wines down the side. The shelves certainly had a good choice. It was then a lady – so heavily pregnant – brushed past. She stared at me in passing with eyes cold and either in protective mode or bordering on the aggressive. I looked away but felt her interest was still in my direction.

I moved down the shop and onto the magazine racks. It must have been at least twenty minutes before the woman came past and went to the counter. I heard her say I will just take a Daily Mail please. I moved around and over to the exit door.

She took her newspaper and sauntered over to the door.

She stared coldly up at me. Are you gonna get outta my way or what – I need to get home – can't you see I am pregnant?

Yes, I said. You have been for the last twelve months or more. Can't you see I am a law upholder?

Now can you see this. It's an aggressive pepper spray. Very useful if faced with conflict.

You know what they can do so get back over there against the wall.

Gingerly with eyes twitching and full of hate, she backed off to the wall.

The lady serving behind the counter came round in protest.

You keep clear for the moment, madam, I said. Your help will soon be needed.

I turned back to Madam Aggression. Now undo that coat, I said. Now! I shouted. That sudden sharp order brought the needed response.

And now undo the blouse... All the way down! I shouted, or this spray wont stop.

The shopkeeper started to protest but then noticed the pregnant one was revealing all.

A pregnant shopping basket for the cost of one newspaper.

Now, I said to the shopkeeper, will you please call the police.

It was my turn for a shock.

I am the police, she said. This lady is now under arrest and will be taken into custody. My colleagues are outside.

Then the door opened and two uniformed officers appeared and cautioned Madam since she had safely given birth, before handcuffing and taking her out.

An elderly lady appeared behind the counter and then I realised that she must be the actual shopkeeper.

Now, Mr Bullen, it is your turn. I need you to come with me to the station where matters will be finalised.

I was taken by the fact that this was unlike normal situations with no attempt made to caution me. That did seem strange but I accompanied the officer on the short drive down to the station.

I am intrigued, I said. How did you know my name is the first question, but then you were already set up at that store. I know no-one locally but surely it can't be a coincidence.

I am Detective inspector Shelley, she said. All will be revealed at the station.

But why haven't you arrested and cautioned me? I said.

I make my own judgements in the line of duty and as I have said: all will be revealed when you are indeed in custody.

With the car parked in the Police compound, DI Shelley led me through reception to her office.

They sat quietly as DI Shelley dealt with some paperwork and then her phone rang.

She answered it quicky then got up and informed me the superintendent was ready to see me.

In total confusion I followed her to his office.

Mr Bullen, Sir, she said and turned to leave.

Superintendent Glassell, he said and motioned me to sit.

Now, Mr Bullen, he said. What have you got to say for yourself?

Well, sir, I said shifting awkwardly in my chair, I am somewhat surprised that I haven't been cautioned and arrested and equally completely bamboozled as to how you tumbled to my latest scheme. And indeed organised your 'witnessing' trap so well.

As you are aware, said Superintendent Glasswell, we as the Police have a very difficult job working along a very fine line. What you have been doing was wrongly applied but with good result. In effect that helped us whilst also hindering us.

We were very lucky in establishing your identity, your history and noting your careful tracking to fulfil your latest success.

We did not openly caution you or arrest you. Your skills were evident from your past security works with the foreign office and those skills could be useful to us.

So my request to you, Mr Bullen, is to stop your solitary efforts but consider working quietly in the background for and with us on similar ventures to the ones you have solved.

Have I clarified the situation?

Perfectly, I said. And I will gladly work under you and assist where I can. That will open my lonesome dull life up again. But – I still have no idea how you not only found me but also my plan of action.

Supt Glasswell held up a finger and made a call out. Send Sergeant Jones in please.

I turned as the door opened and was met with my second shock of the day. Jimmy, I said to a beaming Sergeant Jones. I had no idea you were with the Police.

Plain clothes and keeping work a mystery, chuckled Jimmy.

Well perhaps we can have a quiet beer together and you can fill me in on your Bullen sleuthing activities.

I sure will, he said. If the Super agrees I can drop you off home with a pint and a pie on the way.

With the Super's agreement, he then left the office

Well that's everything all clear now, said Supt Glasswell, and welcome aboard.

I have one question though. That gun you used–is it? Real??

I grinned, stating a boring night with Lego led to a fitting copy being made.

Story 11

A GHOST IN ACTION

N o one would believe that I am a ghost. Although I say it myself I am quite pretty – some men say beautiful. In addition, there is that constant disarming smile. It's that smile – it always fools them.

It's so enjoyable being a ghost. In my life I was fixed on the tales of horror – the tales of the hauntings – and the evils of the dark world.

Those evils I now understand as at one time they were real and those that had suffered them could not sleep.

That is where my story begins.

My parents were always busy and working hard to improve their lives. They were simple people who had never been advised by their parents on finances, ambitions, or even the birds and the bees. As a result, I was equally naïve until I won that scholarship to attend the Girls-only upper school.

The learning curve was swift and quite a shock. It made me see my parents in a different light, but whatever I said or did I could not change them. They were so caring and loving but stuck in a period of time where ambitions were just within the home or connected to the home.

As father enjoyed his Friday nights at the Green Man Pub just down the road – Mother would attend the

Women's Institute. Meanwhile I would be at home getting prepared for a weekend of shopping with the girls and then preparing for the evening dances. On reflection, the shopping with the girls was really a wiggle of hips and a prance around the town, developing a quickly growing trail of young stallions. That trail was to be my downfall.

Aside from the weekend and nightly meets, both myself and the girls were looking at careers. A new life away from school. A way ahead. That very important learning curve of the first step. We got on so well together and steady boyfriends were being developed by some. The dances were noisier than ever with the help of several gin and tonics with mixers gulped down in between.

It is an uneasy time in life when that group of longstanding close friends start to move on and you each find new footpaths to follow in life.

Whilst young a new set of friends is soon formed either at the university in a focussed learning curve or in an office, shop or other place of group employment.

I wasn't a brain box but I was a fun girl and enjoyed life to the full, working in quite a mad estate agents in the town. We were all young at heart with the oldest member being in his thirties. It was very enjoyable with viewings arranged for prospective customers with a high volume of sales meaning no real advertising was needed. The sellers were doing the advertising for us.

We all went out together a couple of times a week and life was good. However as is often the case, something relaxed and enjoyable which has been built up over time can be ruined in a flash.

Although it was a Wednesday and technically supposed to be a quiet day mid-week – it was manic. Gerald the manager was going frantic as Lucy put more calls through to him. We were the only three left in the office. All the others were out attending to viewings.

Lucy turned to me – How are you fixed, Cherry? she asked.

For a viewing now? I said, in some surprise.

Yes, said Lucy. This guy is desperate with his young lady as they like the look of Sparrow Cottage but are flying to Spain in the morning and would like to see it and probably make a decision to purchase today. It's been empty for a while and fully furnished so with the chance of a buyer we need to attend.

He particularly asked for you – said it would be a reunion – but before you ask, in the muddle of the day I never caught his name.

Ok, I said – give me the keys.

Gerald was still on the phone but waved with a smile as I left.

It was three o'clock before I arrived at Sparrow Cottage. There was a car parked outside with a young chap in it. I nodded as I went and unlocked the front door.

I stepped inside and quickly checked the lounge. I had the printout of the rooms and pictures with me, so all was well in hand.

With a tap at the door the young man seen in the car entered. I assume you are Cherry from the agents, he said. My name is Luke.

Hello Luke, I said. Is your lady with you?

No, he said. She had to go to the shops.

There was something about him I did not feel comfortable with.

You don't recognise me, do you? said Luke.

Sorry – no, I replied – should I?

You should really, he said. Me and the lads always met at the dance hall. Sadly, you weren't too interested. But we were.

And as he said that two other lads entered.

And then it started – no matter how I struggled and screamed – there were three of them and I stood no chance.

It was past five-thirty at the Barnes Estate Agents. Gerald stretched and yawned with feet up on his desk. It's been a hell of a day, Lucy, he said.

Yes, she replied – but where the hell is Cherry?

Perhaps she has gone home, said Gerald.

No chance, said Lucy. She has the keys to return and yet to phone in.

Have you tried her mobile? said Gerald.

Many times, said Lucy. Voicemail all the time.

It was Sparrow Cottage, wasn't it? said Gerald. I will go and check it out. It's not far, but a bit remote. She could have broken down. Ok, I will leave now and remind young madam of our closing hours. Are you Ok for half an hour.?

I will survive – a disgruntled Lucy replied.

Gerald backed out of the yard, set his music playing and set himself up for a quick drive down to Sparrow's.

He was surprised on arrival as Cherry's was the only vehicle there and the house was in darkness. He parked up and then checked her car before walking up to the house. The door was open. He stepped inside and called. Switched the light on and moved to the lounge. It was a mess – not like it normally was.

Still calling out, he got his mobile out and rang the office.

Lucy quickly answered.

There is something wrong here in Sparrow Cottage, Gerald said. Her car is the only vehicle outside. The place was in darkness and the lounge is a mess. I am going upstairs.

At the main bedroom he just screamed – and Lucy jumped at the sudden volume of a man's shriek.

Lucy, get the police, get an ambulance – Cherry is in a hell of a state . Nude and bloodied. It's obvious what's happened. My God! My God – no pulse.

The Police arrived – the ambulance arrived – Cherry was dead.

So now I am a ghost and the reason people become ghosts is because there is something in their life that needs to be settled before they can revert to peace.

I have seen my parents distraught.

I have seen the estate agency closed with owners and staff in total shock.

With some joy I have seen the arrests – the legal system in operation and the sentencing. They are now serving time and it is now my turn.

So the three arrogant idiots are in separate prisons. I wonder why that is? Of course, to safeguard against attacks – can't keep the three together, that's for sure – they could defend themselves as a team.

So here I am at the first prison with the first of the three … the leader Luke.

It was midnight. He had a basic cell but the comforts were there. As he slept on his bed, I made sure he soon woke.

Hello Luke, I said.

He awoke then immediately sat up in shock. Cherry – what, how – what are you doing here?

I have come to pay you a visit, I said in the sweetest of replies.

He just sat back in shock.

Now it's time to repeat the enjoyment you must have had, I said – but iit's now my turn. And I will visit you every night until I see the result I want to see... And to make my family and friends very happy.

I moved down towards him then changed my figure to the pose of a horrible witch with fangs and moved in close. He screamed and cried out. The warden came and viewed through the window of his cell then reported that prisoner 243 seemed to be mentally disturbed. No one took any notice. Prisoner 243 was not liked by anybody in the prison – warders included.

Over the course of a few days, I had him shaking – no sleep – and gabbling like he was demented. On the fifth week he was dead and in attendance with Satan shovelling coal.

I repeated the process with the other two with a similar result though one took a while longer.

I now have the option to just return to perfect peace, but I think I will stick around and help others get their revenge.

Story 12

THE PIT – A SOURCE OF LEARNING

It was 1947 and the Second World War had now been over for nearly two years. Industry was picking up. Food rationing was still a controlling factor, but there was a definite buzz with the people – they were relaxed – happy – worry-free and moving forward. Plus actually enjoying working so hard to bring their country back to its original happy state.

The harvest was in full swing – which on hot sunny days always brought the country folk together in the field. Recovery of the corn by that slow old binder had all the village setting up the spilled sheaves of corn into shocks to later get collected by horse and cart for delivery back to the nominated main stack.

Always as the binder closed the central area down with its circular cutting, excitement reigned. The men waiting around the field with sticks at the ready.

Even the ladies had cheeky chuckles as they joined them. It was as if the rabbits knew as each tried to escape in a different direction. Some made it – but some didn't.

So rationing was helped by a delicious rabbit stew.

As time progressed, some wonderful industrial developments were made.

It was 1958 and at last the government cancelled out their control of food rationing.

Horses were replaced by tractors – binders by combine harvesters. The corn on its straw was no longer dropped in tied bundles known as sheaves in the fields and there was no longer the need for the thrashing tackle at the stacks. The combine beat the corn heads off the straw. Then sifted that corn through to a large hopper which when full would offload to a tractor and trailer travelling alongside. The tractor and trailer then returned back to the farm where it tipped its load in the grain pit and quickly returned before the combine tank got too full. The straw was nicely chopped up and laid out in rows across the field as the combine harvester slowly continued on its journey. That straw would be dealt with on a burn up later.

In the barn is a very sophisticated dresser. An auger delivers the corn into it from the pit. The dresser then sorts the corn from the chaff – all electrically powered. A row of sacks are set up in place with different weights set for different corn varieties. Before then tying secure and wheeling away to set up a heap for a lorry to collect later and deliver into the sales.

Jimmy Swann had only just joined the farm as a permanent employee. He loved the farming way of life, being a country lad born and bred. As with his mates the summer holidays were a joy to look forward to. They not only learnt to drive a variety of plant but were paid for it. All managed to work in one of the farms in the area.

Sadly, as a full-time employee he had to now realise his place. He now had to start at the bottom level of the farming duties. In other words, comply with the pecking order – the jobs his seniors were glad to offload.

Each morning he went through training procedures. Charley Hulyer and Barrie Farrow always had two to four hours to work with him and put him right whilst waiting for the crops to dry to a level that the harvesting could start again. The days were then long continuing on until well past nine in the evening, combined with a certain amount of desperation to beat the English weather.

The training procedures were generally just silly banter from the oldies onto the young one and quite enjoyable really. The company was good as Jimmy hated the dresser. The dust was horrendous and the constant low drone through the day brainwashing. Jimmy was badly affected by the corn dust being stuffed up at night and unable to get a good sleep.

Now come on, Jimmy, what corn are we dressing today? said Charley.

Same as yesterday, replied Jimmy quite tartly, bringing a snigger out of a normally very serious Barrie.

And what was that? said Charley ignoring the Jimmy remark.

Same as last week, said Jimmy but shouted out – wheat – as Charley moved across with violence in mind.

And what weight do we bag up the wheat? said Charley.

Eighteen stone, said a very cautious Jimmy.

And if it was barley what would it be then?

Sixteen stone, replied Jimmy, and twenty stone for Black beans.

That brought a nod from both men as sanity had returned.

We will stay with you long enough to empty the pit. It will give you the chance to get a break in the air. There was quite a dag this morning so I think it will be past eleven before we can get combining again.

Jimmy was pleased to hear that and happily copied Charley and Barrie as they kneed the full sacks, grabbed each side and lifted across to the scales. With putting some wheat in or taking some wheat out, the bags were correctly weighed, firmly tied and sack barrowed down to the bottom of the barn in readiness for the lorry to collect.

Barrie and Charley were good to their word and never left until the pit was clear.

A relieved Jimmy grabbed his lunch bag and went round to the calf shed where he was joined by the two terriers – Happy and Heidi – obviously released from their prison in the farmhouse. The housekeeper – Mrs Jacobs – must be in, thought Jimmy. He finished his coffee and a packet of crisps before moving around the farm throwing sticks for the two dogs to collect. They had unlimited energy. Non stop demanding and chasing. As he came to the back of the farm he heard a tractor and realised the fun was over – the corn cart was back in progress.

Barrie reversed back to the pit. Jimmy undid one side of the tailgate while Barrie undid the other. Returning to his tractor and setting the revs before applying the hydraulic lever, Barrie's load was then tipped gracefully down the pit.

Rebolting the tailgate when the trailer returned to normal level, Barrie quickly drove off giving Jimmy a quick wave.

Jimmy switched on the dresser and then the auger. With everything set up the pit slowly emptied … with the indication it was fully empty, but Jimmy realised something was not right. He normally dealt with twenty full bags with some spare. He double checked. It was only sixteen. He checked the dresser internals – all clear – but nothing was being delivered so he guessed the fault must lie within the auger.

He switched the dresser off. Then he switched the auger off and on again… nothing.

So with both switched off he moved around to check the pit.

It was immediately obvious what it was as Jimmy muttered to himself – how the hell did that get down there. A slight woof soon alerted him as the two terriers ran around the corner.

Jimmy clambered down the wall rings and inspected what appeared to be an old coat. It was obviously firmly jamming the auger. He started his move to release it as he heard the tractor arrive.

It had stopped outside the dresser area and Barrie wandered through the open doors. There was no sign of Jimmy, and the auger and dresser were switched off. He has obviously caught up, thought Barrie as he switched both units back on again.

With the noise of the dresser he never heard the scream from Jimmy. His arm was killing him – the coat had been released but replaced by his arm.

He shouted up to Barrie as he undid the side bolts but with the noise of the tractor and the distraction of the two dogs the tail gate was released and the tipping began.

A panic-stricken Jimmy was desperately trying to pull his arm clear but seeing the tipping start he pulled the rest of the coat over his head and steeled himself.

Completely offloaded, Barrie drove off

Returning with his next load Barrie did the normal turn and reverse but could not fail to notice the pit was still quite full from his previous delivery when normally he had to race between keeping the combine tank empty so that could keep going and keeping the pit topped up so the dresser was also kept going.

He walked round to the dresser. It was drumming away but with an obvious lack of dust. The area was eerily deserted.

He called out several times with no reply and checked around the farm. He called to Mrs Jacobs as she was just leaving but she had not seen Jimmy.

With nothing happening at the farm and knowing Charley would be nearly full, he decided to leave everything as it was and take the second tractor and trailer.

On arrival he ran beside the combine and mounted the steps climbing up to put Charley in the know.

Charley stopped the combine to make sure he got the full story.

Well look, he said. It will only take another twenty minutes or so to finish this field. The next field will be Scatters Meadow – the barley. The forecast is not good so we will finish this. Offload my tank and we will return to the farm.

With that agreed they were soon back on the road to the farm.

On arrival back – nothing had changed. Having taken stock of things and in consideration of the time of the day it was agreed to cover the trailers, switch everything off and close up for the night.

It seems there is a fault on the auger, said Charley. Jimmy probably went to see Jim Clayden to get him to look at it.

Let's go – with that and all safely shut up they left.

It was eleven-thirty and Jack and Joan Swann had enjoyed a lovely evening up at the Kings Head Pub.

No sign of Jimmy yet, said Joan. He is usually back by now splashing about in the bath.

Remember where we have been, said Jack – his haunt is the Black Horse so probably well tiddly now. We will leave the downstairs light on.

With that they both retired.

There had been rain in the night and the day looked pretty gloomy.

Jack got up and put the kettle on. Had a quick wash and brush up, made the teas and took one up to Joan.

The light was still on, said Jack.

Have you checked his room? said Joan.

Yes, he is not in, said Jack.

He probably stopped at Mum's, said Joan. Remember! He stayed over there a lot when working on the farm during school holidays and old habits die hard.

That makes sense, said Jack, with us not here last night.

I will make him some special sandwiches and drop them off at the farm later, she said.

Barrie and Charley soon got everything underway but no corn came from the pit.

Have you checked the fuses? said Charley, and where is that damn Jimmy?

The fuses were proven ok.

There is a spare auger in the shed, said Barrie, but we would need to get this one moved off the dresser. We would never be able to remove it as it stands. That other auger may not be working. It's been there so long.

Well it's all we can do until the guvnor returns and gives us his decision.

A voice called out – is anyone there? It was Joan Swann.

Hi Barrie – Hi Charlie – it's so nice to see you. Can you make sure Jimmy gets these, she said. Some sandwiches.

Is he not with you, Joan? said Charlie, without thinking.

No, said Joan. He never came home last night. We assume he stayed with his grandparents.

Again without thinking – have you checked, said Charlie – that he stayed there I mean because we haven't seen him?

Joan looked slightly troubled. I will go round there now, she said, and get back to you. With that she left- – pedalling furiously around the top road to their cottage.

Charley and Barrie got the old auger out of the shed and between them carried it back to the pit. They moved the parked tractor and trailer up to the Dutch barn and struggled across with the auger. They found a spare plug and after a bit of a clean down and a drop of oil in selected places they plugged it in and put it to the test. It performed ok. So the next step was to start dismantling the existing auger.

At that point Joan arrived back.

I am now very worried, she said. He didn't stay at his gran's either. Are you sure he is not here – somewhere? she said.

Charley and Barrie were becoming equally concerned and decided to look further around the farm. Then a shock hit them. His bike was still in the corner of the calf unit where he always left it and his lunch bag and coat on the handlebars.

They returned to Joan in silent harmony. We are as concerned as you, said Charley. Can you check with any of his mates in case he went on a teenage bender with them? We know that is not him but that's why we need to check – what doesn't affect his mates could seriously affect him.

I will, said Joan. And I will get Jack onto it, and we will keep you informed.

As soon as Joan left, the pair got to work on the auger. They were both of the same mind and both seriously concerned… Their biggest fear was…Jimmy was dead.

But God has his ways. As Charley began unbolting the top of the auger from the dresser he heard a sound. He shouted to Barrie. They both stood by the top of the auger and listened. There was sound ... But they could not make out what it was. Then a clear moan came echoing faintly through.

Jimmy – keep calm, shouted Charley. Emergency services are on their way.

The moan continued by return.

Barrie, the farm is locked up and Mrs Jacobs isn't in yet, can you drive round to that telephone kiosk by the post office and dial 999. Explain where we are and ask for ambulance, doctor and the fire brigade.

Why the fire brigade? said Barrie.

Don't argue – they have all the equipment to get him out of this mess.

With that Barrie immediately left.

The emergency services all arrived in good time one after the other.

It was the best decision Charley could ever have made. Once the barrier had been set in place to remove the corn from the area of concern, the fire brigade first cut the auger completely across so Jimmy was now fitted with one steel arm extension. Then the cut down each side to release the auger and Jimmy's arm. A hoist was set up and he was lifted clear and sent to hospital.

As was explained to all by the experts. He was the luckiest person ever to still be alive simply due to having the coat over his head and being close to the bottom of the auger when the corn was offloaded. The force of those tiny grains pushed his face against the bottom of the auger whilst the fabric kept the actual grains clear so he was able to breathe into the angle.

With everyone visiting young Jimmy in – or rather on – his hospital throne, he also had a point to make leaving a very red faced Barrie – but without naming names.

This would never have happened, said Jimmy, had some notices been applied.

I had actually cleared the fault but before I could pull myself clear the motor started up again and dragged me and the garment back in. So – for the sake of health and safety, we must make sure warning notices are put in place whenever equipment is switched off to make it safe to then be worked on.

That rule has – believe it or not – now since been applied across the UK.

Story 13

BUS STOP

As time moves on, advancements are made. Improvements as to how things are done with new tooling ideas produced to assist. As well as the factories, the developments in travel itself moves at speed with land, sea and air records broken annually.

A common factor used at some stage in life by all is the bus or the train. A transport the public rely on whether it be to get to work, get to school or just get to the shops.

Most of the secondary modern or grammar/high schools are set on the edge of the towns or the cities. Country folk rely on the public transport to get their kids safely there.

As the factories such as Ford began to produce more cars so did Optare produce more buses. Designs changed – faster and more efficient models were made with comfort a priority.

The bus moved on from those carefree happy days of the driver and the conductor. The driver shut solidly away in his cab while the conductor – known as the clippy – dealt with the public and their tickets.

With the modern comes more cost, so economies have to be seen to have been allowed for. So now the bus driver has a dual role and is now free from his solitary confinement – he is now both the driver and the clippy – the conductor has gone.

Gerry Hobbs has been a driver now for the past twenty years. He loves his job. Meeting the people, having the banter with the regular shoppers – and then the mad school runs.

His shift this week was the mad school runs but the drive was good. It was a journey on roads across the open fields from one village to the next, picking up the girls for the high school and the boys for the grammar school. Plus any shopper who was brave enough, deaf – or had a pair of ear muffs.

He parked his bike and walked into the depot. Signed in and nodded to James Harris the inspector. He noted his bus had been cleaned – climbed aboard and prepared for his journey.

With a toot and a wave, he was soon on his way. First stop – the village of Caxtowe.

There were a dozen lads and three girls all chattering happily away in the sunshine on the village green. Johny Hubbard was the local farmer's son and very popular as many of the lads joined him on the farm during school holidays. He wasn't really interested in the girls, though Mary Allsop was certainly very interested in him.

As the bus approached, they saw it was Gerry Hobbs driving and they clustered around waiting for the bus door to open. With greetings shared, they all settled in.

Johny took the front seat with his mate Shaun. They had a pocket chess set which they played through each journey. Shaun grinned to himself as he heard Mary Allsop settling in the seat behind them. The rest had all scuttled down to the back seat. Always the most favoured by all was that back seat. Being childish, pulling faces and making signs at the back window to other buses or whatever.

The final pick up was made and it was now the long open journey across the hills to town that remained. Shaun had just called 'Check' to Johny having moved his knight to give the bishop a clear line to the king when the bus suddenly swerved dramatically.

Johny and Shaun quickly looked up as a silent gasp seemed to emanate throughout. Although the road was straight the bus was now mid-road. Johny was concerned.

Are you ok, Gerry? he called but got no reply. He jumped out of his seat as he saw the bus moving faster now and heading for the verge on the wrong side of the road. He immediately saw Gerry was just lying back in his seat as if asleep.

Johny grabbed the wheel and pulled it back whilst yelling to Shaun to come and help.

They had to get Gerry pushed over to get to the ignition key. Johny lay across, telling Shaun with little space left to hold the steering wheel steady.

Johny tried to knock the gears back to neutral with no joy. He pushed on Gerry's leg hard to depress the clutch. Success – he knocked the gear stick back. With revs now roaring they were thankfully free wheeling with Shaun holding the steering wheel. Johny reached down almost under the dash – found the key and switched off the ignition. He moved back up and grabbed the wheel from Shaun and gently pulled the handbrake up. The bus gradually came to a halt with much relief shown all round.

Any traffic travelling along this road would know for sure something was wrong with the bus – the way it was parked at such an angle and with no exit past. But no traffic came.

We have to get him out, said Johny, and called two more lads to help.

Mary joined them and grabbed Gerry's wrist. He has a pulse, she said, but it's very weak. We need to stretch him out to the recovery position but he needs urgent medical help.

Where is the nearest doctor's? said Johny.

The hospital is the only hope, said Mary.

There is no traffic at all using this road, said a desperate Shaun and it's miles on to the hospital.

Move aside, Shaun, said Johny. There is only one thing for it. I have to consider this as a tractor and go for it.

With that he lifted himself over and into the driver's seat. The bus was deadly quiet. Johny made a quick appraisal and started the engine. He had to get the seat forward somehow but perched himself on the edge.

Clutch engaged – gear in place – ease off and move.

Very gently and with high revs sounding, the bus slowly moved forward. Johny was feeling quite sick with the strain of it all but then heard Mary in the background. She was pumping Gerry's chest whilst counting. He remembered then her mother was a nurse so some knowledge was there.

Johny gently moved up into another gear and with a jerk, from his clutch control being poor, the vehicle was moving about twenty miles per hour but soon close to thirty as confidence grew.

This really is the wrong time to hit town, he thought. What could he do? As he steadily continued in second gear along the outskirts of town he saw a telephone kiosk.

He stopped – causing havoc with the traffic – ignoring the fists shaking at him and the horns blowing, he jumped off the bus and entered the kiosk.

He dialled 999 and requested an ambulance urgently to attend the high street – a telephone kiosk outside number 27. The bus will have hazards on.

He got back in the bus and slowly moved it up the road to park on the kerb line to allow the angry traffic to pass. He knelt beside Mary who was still working on Gerry and looking quite exhausted.

Shaun took over from her and Johny gave Mary his handkerchief to clear the sweat from her brow.

It would turn out to be the start of a very close friendship with the mature respect they now had for each other.

The ambulance arrived. Gerry was saved.

The bus with Johny, Shaun and Mary became headlines with a friendly note from the local policeman stating that on this occasion no charges for underage driving would be made.

Many years passed by. Johny stayed with farming and attended the agricultural college.

Shaun joined the fire service and Mary went into nursing. They remained firm friends and Mary Allsop became Mary Hubbard with Shaun their best man.

The times turned hard. Their debt rising with the farm which had become so demanding but never yielding a return they could comfortably live on. After many discussions they both decided it would be better to sell up and regain a life. It took a while to get all plant sold at auction and ultimately get clear. They just got sufficient funds out of the sale once all fees were paid to use as a deposit for a bungalow on the outskirts of Caxtowe.

They were happy but times were very hard and getting harder as the mortgage interest rates rose and the general cost of living was escalating at a great rate of knots. It was inevitable payments were sometimes delayed and they often received warning letters. Their pride would not let them give any indication or make any requests to parents for help.

Whilst Mary continued with her nursing, Johny had become a rep for Rank Animal foods. He actually quite liked his job. A car with expenses was part of his package and he enjoyed meeting up again with all the farmers he knew from his earlier days. They were certainly supportive with any needs they had always put his way.

It was mid-week and Johny pulled up to the side of the garage, noting that Mary was already home.

As content as he had been through the day, the look on Mary's face was indicative of something not right.

He went up to her. I haven't seen you like this for ages, he said. What's wrong?

You know we are behind with our mortgage, said Mary. Well, there is a letter there from the solicitors. I haven't opened it but my instinct tells me it is serious.

Johny quickly opened the letter.

It is from Michael Cohen-Jones, he said. He has asked if we could attend his offices at 10am tomorrow.

It sounds urgent, agreed, but he has always looked after us. He knows our business better than we do. I think we must go.

Mary nodded – Yes, let's get it over with – sooner rather than later.

The next morning at 9.45 they both reported in at Parkere Knowles – the town solicitors. They were soon ushered up to Michael Cohen-Jones' office, who greeted them with his normal pleasantries.

As you are no doubt aware this visit must hold something of great importance as I don't believe you have been summoned here before. Forgive that terminology, he said with a grin.

Mary was beginning to shake.

Now, he said, I have some very sad news for you. You remember a gentleman – Gerry Hobbs. They both nodded. Well sadly he passed away last week.

Mary turned to Johny and grabbed his hand with them both remembering that journey on the bus.

Well, continued Michael Cohen-Jones. He left a will.

In that will is his house and quite a sizeable bank account.

He has bequeathed that to you both – in his words: As the two youngsters to whom I owe my life – may this now help them through theirs.

The two were in shock.

Michael Cohen-Jones had known them so long and knew the life struggles they had been going through so he could not resist getting out of his chair and risking being drowned in their tears as he gave them both a handshake and hug.

In fact, his eyes were watering too which never happens with the legal profession.

Story 14

A LUCKY ESCAPE

T he Roberts family lived in a small Suffolk village with the East Anglian capital of horseracing close by. Geoff had met his wife Tracey at a youth club in Newmarket and their relationship quickly developed with Saturdays at the dances and Sundays in the cinema – missing most of the film.

The town was always full of life with the stable lads running riot against the American servicemen visiting from their air bases of Lakenheath and Mildenhall.

Geoff and Tracey had a quiet wedding in June 1979 and continued with a honeymoon journey by train and ferry to the Isle of Wight. That certainly was some honeymoon spent at the Berry Brow hotel which catered perfectly for newlyweds. Nine months later that was evident when their daughter Chrissy was born.

They had worked hard together saving hard to build up a deposit to buy their first home. But times were tough with the cost of living escalating.

Geoff worked in a small splinter section of a large civils contractor that had won a massive contract to lay a network of main feeder pipelines across the UK introducing Natural Gas for the population. Those pipelines emanating from Bacton in Norfolk would cross the country into new compresser stations, where the gas was subject to pressure controls, allowing it to serve the domestic fraternity.

The splinter section worked out designs for preserving what was a dangerously high pressure network of gas against natural external corrosion attack. The lines obviously passed through many different types of soil and water with a vast difference in electrical resistance. Their aim in design was to develop systems to raise the pipes' electrical levels both uniform and to safe margins.

The company was operating worldwide which was now a boom period. They won similar projects in Libya and Saudia Arabia.

After much discussion between Geoff and Tracey he signed a contract on tax free double pay to work direct for the Libyan Oil company 'Oil Plus' on a six-week out, two-week home agreement. The annual field break time would break the sixty-three day tax-free rule so they had booked a holiday in Malta each autumn.

With a great deal of sadness Geoff packed his bag to return on his next stint. His next field break would see him home for Christmas – making that 1985 event unforgettable.

He hugged Tracey and held a tearful Chrissie pleading with him not to go. With tears in his eyes he turned and went straight to the check-in desk.

The plane landed safely with two trucks and the army waiting by the runway.

Geoff gazed through the small porthole window of the Fokker Friendship F27 plane wondering why the army were always there.

This was the desert. This was a desert camp in the middle of the Sahara – the middle of nowhere. He accepted his were not the reasons to consider why as he collected his bag from the rack and stumbled along the gangway to leave the plane.

The maintenance manager wants to see you, said Claude Philby.

Well I wonder what his problem is – it won't be a social call or a welcome back, that's for sure, I replied. When did he ring?

About an hour ago.

Ok I better get round there – he is bound to have spotted my vehicle and know that I am back. Mustn't keep his Lordship waiting.

It never ceased to amaze me how the Libyan managers' desks were always so clear. Not a paper on them. It seems that once qualified – that is it. Nonetheless, men are doing their required duties so perhaps we should learn the psychology to then follow their example.

Good morning, Muhammed, Kaif Harlech – I said.

Qwais Humdelelah, all is good, replied Muhammed. Take a seat Mr Geoff, he said. We have lots to discuss.

Firstly, we need your report for the cp systems serving the tank farm.

Secondly, they need you to meet them up at the Gas plant to determine the needs to protect their buried plant up there.

However, my main concern is the fuel line to the air strip.

There is no problem with the first two, I replied. But the third one is a worry.

I warned them all about that pipeline many months ago when they were complaining at having to attend to a leak at least once a month – and at all hours. It does need a power impressed system applied to it and fast, BUT – and I stress this point – if they get leaks now, say each month, they will get many leaks in a very short space of time after the pipeline has polarised but then none at all after that – and whilst the system is kept running of course.

How can that be? said Muhammed. You have installed something to preserve the pipeline but then it leaks more. That does not make any sense to me.

I understand exactly what you are saying, Muhammed, I said, but this is what people in general cannot understand.

The pipe has sat there for many years with probably a sub-standard coating and no other protection. So it is allowed to just rust freely.

We suddenly introduce an electrical system which changes the haphazard DC voltage levels that naturally exist along the length of that pipeline. It converts that naturally occurring situation to one controlled with total uniformity. But –whilst this action preserves the pipe from further harm, it first cleans the pipe down. That is the best way I can describe it. So, any rust is in fact lifted and of course where it is really bad it then results in the oil leakage.

All the bad areas that are currently in various stages of revealing themselves will now all occur pretty much at the same time.

So if I design and get a system installed now – they will want to kill me in say two months' time. But if still alive they will be happy and I will get the occasional smile with there being no call outs later on.

Ok, said Muhammed. I think I understand the points you have made. In reality, the protective coating is no good and should never have been applied.

No – the coating is the first line of defence, but because of the damage caused to it during the laying of the pipeline not being repaired, then the pipe at that point is bare, exposed and open to concentrated corrosion attack.

So I will make out the order now to get things moving, said Muhammed. How soon can you action it all is the question.

The materials will take at least ten to twelve weeks to get here but say all will be in place and commissioned within four months.

That's settled then. I leave it all in your capable hands, said Muhammed.

With that Geoff dismissed himself, bid his farewell and left the office.

Geoff found the old drawings and extracted the detail he needed. The total length of line and diameter. He calculated out the external surface area of the pipe and applied what he considered could be the total needed to preserve the whole pipeline with it isolated off at each end.

Materials listed and passed across for management to order left Geoff to get the siting of an earth bed agreed and a suitable AC power supply for a permanently mounted Transformer rectifier.

Geoff and his family had a wonderful Christmas. New year's was personally stressful as getting close to his time for return to the desert.

It was the normal chaos at Tripoli airport getting the connection across to Benghazi followed by the flight back to camp the following day.

The materials had all arrived and the installation work soon commenced. All went well with a small rig getting down to the shallow water table with the anodes and backfill swiftly applied.

All wired and commissioned with the pipeline now changed from a row of potentials ranging from -0.5 volts DC to -0.76 volts now depressed to an even -1.2v.

Geoff once again warned everyone to be prepared for a flurry of leaks before it settled back to no leaks once those were repaired.

Returning back from his second leave he arrived back on site late March.

They were generally happy with things with there being just the one leak in the interim and that was in the daylight hours. So Geoff relaxed and settled back into his maintenance routines.

Unbeknown to anyone working in the desert, reprisals were now being actioned by the United States Government against Colonel Gaddafi following a number of incidents conducted by the Libyans against the American servicemen. The final straw being a serious attack on the servicemen again but this time at a discotheque in West Berlin.

With no possibility of telephone or any other means of contact, Tracey had been monitoring events closely. Then on the 15th April 1986 Tracey was screaming her head off and waving her fist furiously at the ceiling as warplanes from the Lakenheath and Mildenhall air bases flew over.

President Ronald Reagan had said enough is enough and both Tripoli and Benghazi suffered bombing raids.

In the UK there was some concern flagged up regarding the five thousand oil and gas workers now stranded in Libya. A firm and uncompromising Margaret Thatcher was quite adamant in her response – They knew the risk – it's their problem.

Whilst Tracey was beside herself with worry the oilfield was in fact quite remote from all the troubles. They heard of it of course and were confined to camp – that is, until a flurry of oil leaks occurred on the airstrip fuel line. Together with an army escort the crews worked tirelessly to carry out the repairs without reference to Geoff with the acceptance of his early concerns – his early fears and warnings and with the tensions around them no reference to Geoff was made.

However, Geoff was in for a shock as the door of his chalet was pounded hard the following morning. On opening, he was dragged out by the army and marched to the office. And there the extent of his fear was developed further with the accusation of sabotage to prevent use of the air pad.

In angry denial he referenced the Maintenance manager Muhammed as the approver of his work.

Only to be informed that he had also been arrested.

With arms tied he was taken to the air strip and pushed onto a waiting plane which immediately turned for take off.

He overheard the pilot stating Tobruk and felt some relief in knowing it was not to be Benghazi or Tripoli because of the American bombings, but instead the place he was most familiar with.

He was somewhat relieved to think he knew Libya so well. His first journey out had been on the Zuetina oil terminal where he travelled down from Benghazi by road via Adgee Dhabia.

Then – involved with managing the works from Tobruk down to the Booster Station and onwards across the sand sea to Sarir.

Whilst he knew the locals would all be scared of their army – he knew that somehow they would see a way to help him. And they did.

He had been locked in a room for three days with brief escorts to the Captain's office to be questioned. Pretty useless being questioned by one who does not understand English.

On the fourth day his room was unlocked but in shock he recognised the man before him who smiled and put finger to lips but withdrew a note that he placed on the tray and then left.

Geoff kept himself calm. The note held his escape route to freedom but not before vast effort was made with great risks attached.

It said: You have your watch – door unlocked; leave at three. Keys in Land Rover in yard. Cross by the cones to Egypt.

Geoff made sure the note was destroyed and waited. It seemed an age but when three came he tentatively tested the door. It was unlocked – he quietly opened it and crept to the stairs. Ran swiftly down and out carefully to the yard.

The Land Rover was there. He climbed inside – the keys were in place and he quickly started the engine and left. The tension was horrific but the thought of being executed as a spy or a traitor overcame everything else. As he left the main town and ventured off the main road to cross the rough limestone-packed desert he felt more relaxed and followed the main oil line, which he had worked on a year or so back. Then on down towards the Booster Station before swinging across to the Egyptian border. To locate where Gaddaffi had set up a safe point of access painted to identify a clear access point into Egypt.

This was where great alertness and care was needed. There was an old minefield left by the British from the Second World War. Gaddaffi had asked for help to make it safe but to no avail. He then had put barriers up along the Egyptian border with his own mines when they had refused to merge across with them. The laugh was the painted area that signified safe entry should his army need to invade Egypt. All quite simply crazy but sadly a true fact.

With vehicle lights approaching in numbers still in the distance he had to find it.

The paint had faded but he thought it must be the place. He had no option as the vehicles were fast approaching and he feared may open fire. He drove straight for it and gritted his teeth. With a loud crash that barrier gave way and he was through – but where to go now? He certainly had never been this side before.

As his mind was focussed on compass bearings, he had a good idea how far down he was and where to head. He need not have worried but now more lights were racing towards him and now he was surrounded. With hands held high he stepped down from the vehicle.

Then came a pleasant surprise as a voice rang out – Mr Geoff, what took you so long. It was an old colleague from Cairo who had worked with him on the main oil line. They hugged quite dramatically as he said Ahmed had given him a call, filling him in with the full story and to help the escape.

Geoff could not believe his luck and how earlier friends and acquaintances could mean so much.

Geoff spent a few days in Cairo, needing a new passport from the British embassy there.

The bombing paled into insignificance as on April 26th the great Chernobyl Nuclear plant blew up in Ukraine. That explained all the dead swallows that littered the area now – they must have flown through it all.

Then on April 30th having been interrogated by the British Foreign Office, Geoff returned home to a relieved Tracey and an ecstatic Chrissie.

Having had such an experience and received some publicity and fame, Geoff was never intending to travel again. Much to the joy of his family.

Story 15

DEVIL'S PIT

As I sat in front of the telly dozing, I suddenly woke up with a start. I just could not believe what I was seeing – it was that James Pinkerton-Conway applying to a team of professional business entrepreneurs for finance to support him with his new invention. He never invented anything.

I just could not believe it. The front – the lies – an absolute conman.

Luckily, the group seemed to become aware on an independent basis that something wasn't right. He was dismissed with no investor but on leaving told the camera crew that he did not need the money – he needed the publicity.

He had made no mention of his other companies, their failures and how he depended on ruining the small elders trying to retire, by ripping false fees with legal threats off them as he had promised to sell their company.

I had been hit hard by him with his failed promises to sell my company. With no buyer in sight after more than a year and with his colleagues' agreement and our accountants' advice we transferred the company within family. There had been months of legal fees when there had been only trivials interested who clearly did not have the funding.

As with many small businesses who transferred within family, we got hit with legal threats from Mr Conman. Even though no action had been taken without prior agreement of Mr Conman's co-director that after a year's grace we would get together and try again.

Being small, I was advised to pay as court fees would be high and run on for possibly years.

So with all the earlier pain brought to the surface again I poured myself a treble whisky and switched the annoying television off.

As I climbed the stairs I vowed to myself that if I got an incurable disease, I would hunt that beast down and make sure no one else got hurt.

The drink took its desired hold and sleep beckoned.

The next hours were total confusion.

Was it a dream – was it really happening – was it a nightmare? It became clearer as the events unfolded.

Tossing and turning – followed by three trips to the toilet – then at last, sleep took over.

I awoke in a darkened room. It felt strange the way the light gradually improved, revealing a bench with four beings quietly sitting there and studying me.

Then one stood up. Difficult to properly see features but cloaked, tall and slim.

I am Satan and you are now welcomed to our home – the Devil's Pit.

I know you are Roger but I need to be sure what it is you actually require from us so let me introduce you to my colleagues. Starting from the left is The Devil; next to him – Lucifer. Then Beezlebub and finally The Prince of

Darkness. Now inform us of your needs and a judgement will be made.

Right – this is it – no holds barred.

I have been the subject of evil. Something developed by you.

I want that corrected. So I have formed a company called 'Grudge Repairs Unlimited'.

Its purpose is to reverse the pain given under your guidance and control to innocent people and hit back at those imposing it – and with some venom.

I am asking for just two bags of coal for a fifty per cent share in my business and your help to reverse the problems that you must have instigated in the first place.

It all went quiet – the room faded back to darkness and perfect peace followed.

It was early morning, not quite light but the need for tea was calling. I put on my dressing gown and carefully went downstairs and put the kettle on. As I sat sipping, some recollection of the night returned with the realization that whisky and nightmares seem to suddenly work in tandem with one another .

Since that damn television show had revised the hate that once again dominated my mind, I knew I had to do something. I am fit still but past eighty so need to do something now whilst still able.

I found Mr Conman's company details and searched for addresses on the Government's Companies House site. A bit unsure, I rang the company and yes he was still the MD. I then broached the subject of setting up a possible meeting with him but was advised that he was very busy and could only consider serious investors. I exaggerated an Arabic twang to my voice, stating very firmly I was travelling back to Saudi Arabia on Saturday, but if he wasn't interested in serious funds being available I would find another interested party. Finishing by stating the start of a curt goodbye brought an interrupted no wait, sir, please wait, I will see what times are available.

With a time and day agreed, I prepared myself to journey down to Dover. I was on a spying mission.

I waited in clear view of his office and then saw him.

He was just getting in a vehicle. With some relief I could see it was his Mercedes as there was no-one else near the car.

A plan was forming in my mind. I needed to get him away from office and away from town. Somewhere quiet was a must.

Many thoughts and considerations considered. I resigned myself to the fact I would be spending the rest of my days in a very special care home – HM Prison.

As once the matter had been dealt with, I would give myself up.

I returned to the hotel and put plan B into operation.

The aim was that I would contact his office again tomorrow and state I was in Dover but could only now meet in the evening. I would suggest the quiet seating area at the top of the cliffs would be an ideal spot this time of the year– then request her to arrange for him to meet me there where we can have a quiet discussion to see if my million or two investment is of interest – if so we can move down to the Glow Worm hotel and have dinner together.

After a brief call – the secretary confirmed he would meet me there at 7pm. I told her I would have my hazard lights on if he could do the same. With that in place I commenced my rehearsal of plan B.

I would get there early and set my vehicle up. Then just before seven – as I knew he was a stickler for time – I would move across in the dark and get comfortable to then just wait. On arrival he would become impatient and walk over to my vehicle. I would then sneak over and set his vehicle up so he would never reach the Glow Worm Hotel.

I arrived up at the cliffs at 6.30. Set my vehicle facing back down the hill. Walked over and found a nice seat with good cover surrounded with some sparse shrubbery. Never would have thought a set up could be so perfect.

With a quarter of an hour to go I set the hazards up – got out of my car again and moved over to the seat and waited.

Waited …and waited. It must be gone seven now I thought when blue lights appeared from nowhere and a police car arrived. They got out and walked over to my car. I cautiously got up and walked over to them.

Sorry got took short, I said, pretending to rezip the flies.

You left your hazards on Sir. Was there any reason for that?.

Yes, I said. I had a meeting arranged here for 7pm before continuing on for a meal somewhere. Difficult to be sure who you are meeting in the dark.

Well that is very true, Sir, said the first officer.

You were here to meet Mr James Pinkerton-Conway, we believe.

That is true, I said with some surprise. We were supposed to meet up at seven to discuss a business deal.

That confirms what his secretary told us. Sadly, you won't be meeting Mr Pinkerton-Conway, Sir. It seems he had a new automatic Mercedes Benz which he had not got familiar with and roared off in reverse gear over the edge of the cliff when parking – not the forward gear. They are recovering him now from the base of the cliff. It seems he also got the time set up wrong on his watch … An hour fast.

I sat down in the front of my car in shock. I confirmed to the officers that I was ok and they left.

There was no point staying down in Devon, so I settled up with the hotel and left. They were aware of the circumstances which had it seemed gone viral.

It was quite late before I arrived home but a double whisky did the trick again and the bed summoned.

Then it started all over again.

Was it a dream – was it a nightmare … or was it really happening?

I was back in the darkened room, but this time there was only Satan there.

Well you should be happy now, he said.

We have corrected your grudge having been told firmly – and clearly put in our place.

But that debt has now been settled.

So, enjoy what time you have left, Roger, and goodnight. The room was black again.

Waking with a start it was another whisky that beckoned – not tea this time but – time for a private celebration.

Story 16

WALNUTS AND SQUIRRELS – THE WALNUT TREE

Hazel was at the kitchen sink washing up. Her daughter Rachel was beside her doing the drying. It was more or less a Sunday morning ritual when she was home from College.

There they are again, Mum, she said as two squirrels raced around and up the old walnut tree – their home and their fun palace.

I love them. When I sit in the study doing my art stuff there is always a tap on the window and there sits Sandy Squirrel with hand outstretched. I open the window and she grabs my finger and with the other arm grabs the hazel nut I have ready and then off she runs. I do love them.

Well, take my advice and don't mention them to your father. He hates them.

At that moment there was a loud bang which seemed to come from upstairs.

My God – what's happened. Look, said Rachel. A squirrel has just fallen out of the tree and is just twitching around on the ground. Looks to be in dreadful pain. I must go to him.

Hazel quickly moved from the sink and with her wet hands grabbed Rachel by the shoulders. She looked intensely at her, demanding she stays in the house.

It's your father, she said. He has had his shotgun licence renewed and now deals with what he considers is the vermin.

Sadly I have to agree with him. He is right, they are vermin and carry nasty diseases as well as being very, very destructive.

Rachel could not believe what she was hearing and just shook her head and sat down at the kitchen table.

The Bixbys had not long moved into their new home. With the old walnut tree dominating the edge of the back garden they were considering renaming the address to 'Walnut Tree Towers'. The tree was protected by a conservation order but not protected by anything else.

The walnuts produced were beautiful and very enjoyable. The first year they collected many bowlfuls and saved some for Christmas but gave many to friends and family. That was last year. Obviously, the previous owners had controlled the squirrel population – not so this year. So, Mark Bixby got to work.

Traps were tried, an air gun was useless, so a shotgun licence was applied for. With a supposedly silenced 4.10 single barrel Mark would wait upstairs with gun at the ready by the bathroom window as it was an ideal position overlooking the tree.

It really was quite amazing. With one family shot, another family would immediately move in. It could almost be imagined that a queue was waiting with cases ready at the bottom of the garden.

So far, the toll was eighteen squirrels killed and removed. It almost became a sport for Mark as even sitting in the lounge he would spot a squirrel and race upstairs to the bathroom. But he had to be very careful how he moved the barrel out of the bathroom window. Those animals were not stupid. But even as a hunter he could not understand the lack of love between the animals. Two playing together on the lawn would indicate a relationship of some kind. One gets shot – the other just carries on playing as if nothing has happened. Happily, leaves the playmate and toddles further up the garden and back to the tree. No love and no concern shown. A very cold and weird attitude.

I can't believe you, Dad, said Rachel at tea that night. You are so kind and loving – you look after us all but then you show a murderous side killing those lovely squirrels.

I agree with you seeing them as lovely, said Mark. I used to feed them and happily watch their antics when your mother and I were first married. We even set up challenging and difficult courses for them to get to a selection of their special food. The more difficult we made it they always eventually cracked it and got to the food. We had a lot of fun with them in those days.

But things changed. They began to dominate the garden and destroy bird feeders and they were so greedy.

Then with their disease and ferocity the dear young red squirrel vanished. But now, besides the flood of grey squirrels we now have bigger and more ferocious black squirrels.

Ok, said Rachel, but can you stop your murderous antics at weekends when I am home and holidays so I don't see the carnage you cause. I understand about the reds – I believe they are being cared for up North where the aim is to get them breeding in numbers again. I haven't seen a black squirrel and don't really want to if I am honest.

Mark agreed with some reluctance and Hazel gave Rachel a sly wink.

Daddy looking after little daughter again, she muttered – the favoured one – a nice relaxed bonding feel emanated around the table.

The college had broken up for the Christmas holidays. It was a pleasant time with Rachel back home and friendly reunions down the pub as a family.

That evening Rachel was lying quietly in her bed reading when she heard a noise above. She put her book down and listened. There it was again. It sounded like scratching. She put her dressing gown on and crept across to her parents' bedroom. Dad, she whispered – Dad.

Hazel woke up and looked at her with concern.

What's wrong Rachel? she said. Tapping Mark hard to wake him.

There is something scratching away above the ceiling in my room, said Rachel.

Both Mark and Hazel got up and followed her to her room where they all sat on the bed and waited.

Sure enough – after five minutes it started up again and quite intense.

Probably mice, said Hazel.

Too loud for mice, said Mark. I bet it's a damn rat.

I will get in the loft in the morning and check it out and put some poison down.

With that they all retired, and Rachel put the pillow over her head and went to sleep.

Not for long – as she woke with a start. Something had happened but she had no idea what it was so put the light on. There was no light. And with the cold she switched on her heater but that didn't work either.

She daren't wake her parents up again so pulled the covers tightly up and eventually got warm enough to resume her sleep.

At breakfast they discussed the happenings of the night.

I have no electric in my room, said Rachel.

Yours was built on later, said Mark, and has a separate circuit. The last owners had that part set up for their elderly mother.

We decided it was ideal so we could lock you away – that was mainly what attracted us to make the purchase.

Oh ha ha, said Rachel as Hazel could not resist an agreed nod and giggle.

Anyway – I will leave you two to clear the table and wash up while I get the steps and get that loft checked out, Mark said.

The two ladies were still in the kitchen when they heard ripples of laughter coming from Rachel's room.

They moved over to her room and saw Mark's head looking down from the loft.

Would you like to join me up here, Rachel, he said.

With some confused reluctance but with her mother's help, Rachel climbed the steps.

Now follow my light, said Mark.

You can see over there, there has been a lot of destruction. All seemingly caused by gnawings.

Oh yes, said Rachel. That's terrible. Is that damage repairable – or rather how long do you think it will take to put right? she asked.

Mark moved the light over, ignoring her question.

Oh and look who has done that for you, he said.

She gasped … And could not believe her eyes. It was a pair of grey squirrels.

So, said Mark. Once I have found and blocked wherever they got in this time I will get the repairs done.

Then I am sure you will welcome your first lesson in using a shotgun in the garden… and stop laughing, Hazel, please.

Story 17

WHO SAID THE LAW IS AN ASS.

T he office was quite quiet as they all had their heads down working but the atmosphere was happy as normal. Everyone got on well together and supported one another with all work covered when anyone was off for whatever reason.

The workload was quite heavy as the end of the financial year was approaching. It was always the same. It seemed that all the big conglomerates suddenly came to life with the realisation there remained excess funds to be spent if the new budget was to be a healthy one.

In a lot of ways – whilst considered a small company – it was unique in its specialised field. The employees were equally unique with both their dedication and strong bonds of trust and friendship.

That had emanated through a variety of individual hardships suffered when the industry went downhill with many made redundant from the major companies. The Middle East troubles being the main cause.

John Smith and his wife Pamela were not too concerned, but with the loss of those lucrative overseas projects and a swift redundancy notice, John needed to find work. He contacted the few specialist companies that he knew. Staff were known to him at each place and were generally friendly and sympathetic. However, not so the last one which drew venom and purpose out of him. The manager of that company rudely interrupted the interview to ask if they had got all the information out of him that was needed. If so – let him go.

John and Pam struggled along for a little while before agreeing to set up a company of their own and effectively become self-employed. It was to be a big learning curve, but John's friends from within the gas and the oil companies soon gave him work. The Middle East then surprised him by redirecting their buying houses in London to buy their CP material needs through his company.

The company soon grew and within a few years The Metal Preservers Ltd was well established and registered with the majors and employing a crew of twenty-five people.

John called out to Jimmy Day. Who is dealing with the Esso surveys?

Colin Jackson is doing the North. I am looking after the East, he replied.

Oh, how long will the East take then? said a very happy sounding Joe Halliday.

About two weeks, said Jimmy. And don't sound so flipping happy about it.

Pam giggled. He just knows that a wonderful peace will reign over us, she said.

Jimmy snorted but said nothing.

As happens in life things go downhill. But it was not the work itself, it was Pamela. She hadn't been feeling well of late and with a number of tests made, cancer of the breast was proven.

She had weeks of chemotherapy and was currently bed bound. With the seriousness of the situation her daughter Katherine left her job to join The Preservers.

It was a doubly tough time for John as Pam covered all the admin side and John knew nothing about vehicle renewal dates for tax/ MOT or insurance. Equally when rent or rates were due.

He contacted the vehicle insurers they used and they visited. It turned out all the renewals were at different times. John wanted to do the lot as one blanket insurance, but the young lad was against that idea, stating that he should just wait and renew as necessary. So that was how it was left.

Three weeks passed. Pam was no better. Very weak and very tearful, which is understandable for a normally fit and busy person.

The phones in the office had been quite busy, but the site reports and invoicing was quietly moving along. That soon changed.

The phone on Pam's desk rang. John moved across and took the call. It was a very distraught Jimmy. Boss, I've been stopped by the police. No insurance. Not allowed to drive. I will get banned, I know it.

Now calm down, Jimmy. Where are you?

Near the Colchester turn off.

Right stay there – is the officer with you?

Yes, said Jimmy.

Let me speak with him please – and Jimmy – just calm down.

John explained the situation with the officer. Stating all the vehicles on the books and how Pam normally dealt with it all, but sudden illness left us vulnerable.

The policeman was very understanding and quite sympathetic with similar suffering himself but with his young lad.

I will wait here, he said, while you get your broker onto it. Then once I know it's insured he can drive back. However, it will go to court. I can't help with that as it automatically reported into Swansea.

Ok, I said – and thank you.

John got through to the broker. The insurance was renewed and Jimmy allowed to drive back to the office.

It was three weeks later the summons came to attend the magistrate's court.

The policeman involved visited and was greatly sympathetic but could do nothing other than be officious. He said, I shall be in court so don't worry.

I had taken the rap for Jimmy although really he should be the one as the driver takes responsibility for the vehicle he drives. I couldn't see him suffer with the dire panic he had shown. His fear was justified as he only needed three more points on his licence to face a ban.

I wrote in with an explanation but got nowhere.

With a solicitor in attendance I attended the court.

The situation was explained but they awarded me seven points which with the six I already had took it over the set level of twelve.

With that a young barrister still wearing nappies jumped up from the front shouting ban him for twelve months.

I was in total shock. This was ludicrous.

My solicitor just stated we shall be lodging an appeal and we left the court.

The office thought I was joking. I angrily responded that it was no joke.

The crazy part was hearing in the news that a man had 51 points on his licence but was still allowed to drive as his family depended on him. Unbelievable.

It was the appeal time. It seemed the judge had to stay with some of the decision. He opted to reduce the seven points down to six bringing it to an equal twelve.

Then spoke quite friendly saying you work long hours and travel long distances and need a rest.

I ban you for one month.

That in itself was a relief but I really could not see it.

I myself have always been insured. This was a company issue through circumstances and at worst I would have expected the company to have been fined something like £2000.

The fifty-oner was caught again – and this time was banned.

Whoever made that statement that the law is an ass should be knighted.

ODES

IT'S OPENING TIME – A MODERN FRUSTRATION

I have a bottle
It is full of sauce
With a use by date
In big letters of course.

Now comes the challenge
To access to use
Then beat the date
With tempered abuse.

I have another bottle
It is full of shampoo
But how to enter
I wish I knew.

Now there is the milk
Capped green, blue or red
So simple the screw top
But fingers then bled.

Its heat sealed in silver
With very small lip
Need pliers on standby
And a first aid kit

My ready made meal
Was microwave bound
With all sleeving removed
And film pierced all round

Four minutes later
With one left to stand
Try removing the cover
Without burning the hand.

Preservation is a must
Security the need
But please – I am old
For simpleness I plead.

So apart from needing
A university degree
In the opening of bottles
Or simply setting stuff free

Just read the instructions
Be prepared for a puzzle
Have light tools on standby
And a calmer to guzzle.

TIME

Time is against us – no matter what
It drags its heels when we're in a spot
Then when we need it to help us through
We make the excuse – well time just flew
Love is the spark that keeps life advancing
As passion develops and males start their prancing
A bond soon develops with unification
Then a home is set up with domestication.
New life emerges in less than a year
We nurture and cherish with laughter and tear
Then time has its way and we fade away
Leaving those we created to mourn on the day.
So no matter what – we may be the host
But we have no control over what matters most
In the lottery of life – no matter the breed
Time is the winner – longevity the need.

THE WALNUT TREE.

First come the leaves
Or is it the breeze
That kick starts the life in this tree.

For life it withstands
With many a band
Of squirrel and others with fleas

I take it on board
The squirrels' big hoard
Of fruits that they gather with ease

For now that old tree
Has a large family
As it stands there so happy to please.

But then seasons pass
And nuts fall to grass
Wild siblings cough and sneeze

And with winter near
The leaves disappear
So cooling the 'birds and the bees'.

So where we are now
Is close to the plough
As sleep beckons the deciduous trees.

But this tree is lucky
With a guard that's so plucky
With ET now taking a bough.